LUNADAR

HOMEWARD BOUND

DONNA L MARTIN

Story Catcher Publishing
Knoxville, Tennessee

Donna L Martin/Story Catcher Publishing
P O Box 27788
Knoxville, Tennessee 37927

www.donnalmartin.com

Publisher's Note: This is a work of fiction. Names, characters, places, and incidents are a product of the author's imagination. Locales and public names are sometimes used for atmospheric purposes. Any resemblance to actual people, living or dead, or to businesses, companies, events, institutions, or locales is completely coincidental.

Book Cover Design by Nimra Junaid.

LUNADAR: Homeward Bound/Donna L Martin 2nd edition.

ISBN 978-1-7323278-0-1 (ebook)
ISBN 978-1-7323278-1-8 (print)

Dedicated to my friend and editor, Steve Patterson, for seeing my Lunadar vision and helping me breathe life into my story.

If there is a book you want to read, but it hasn't been written yet, you must be the one to write it

—TONI MORRISON

ACKNOWLEDGMENTS

This book could not have been possible without a group of supportive people who believed in the story of Lunadar and its people.

Thank you to Nimra Junaid, artist extraordinaire, for creating such lovely book covers for this LUNADAR trilogy.

Thank you, Shahbaz Awan, for your years of dedication as my production manager at Story Catcher Publishing. I never have to worry about formatting as long as you are in my corner.

Thanks to my son, Randy Martin, for his expertise in what constitutes fantasy realms, after years of reading in that genre.

And, finally, thanks to my sister, Janet Lavergne, who was possibly my biggest fan while on this Earth, and who is probably still cheering me on my author journey from wherever her spirit now resides.

TESTIMONIALS

"This is not a genre I usually read much of, however I thoroughly enjoyed this book. The story moved along at great pace while hinting at unresolved secrets and leaving you wondering how they would be revealed." (Christine Amazon 4-star review)

"I love adventure and survival stories. This book has both. The downside to Lunadar is one must wait for the next book to see what happens with Ariana and Candra." (Janet Amazon 5-star review)

"I LOVED the storyline!! I kept wanting to know more about what adventure would lead Ariana to her next challenge of survival or defeat." (Paula Amazon 5-star review)

The World of Luhndar
WESTERLY WATERS
TARI BAY
NORLAC WATERS
LORD SHEPAK'S CASTLE
ALVERAK
TALI BAY
TURO MOUNTAINS
QUALLAN FOREST
SULLACK SEA
DREY DAK'S FALLS
SOUTHERN SEAS
RENNDAR
N
W
E
S

TABLE OF CONTENTS

CHAPTER ONE

The setting sun bathed the deck in an unnatural light. The men were restless. Too long from land, too long from home and it weighed heavily upon their spirits. This night would be a rough one with choppy seas and razor-sharp tongues. Princess Ariana's hand gripped the railing and her body swayed in rhythm to the waves. Her eyes peered into the fading light as if to see land just beyond the portal. She would get no rest that night.

Voices wafted up from below, a harsh word muttered here and there as men settled down in cramped quarters reeking of sweat and dirt from many days at sea with only the moonlight for company. Ariana's body begged for rest, but her mind raced. Crowded with the what-ifs and what-could-have-been of another lifetime. Too late to change things. The sea called to her, and she was forced to follow the moon.

Ariana struggled to stay awake. Many depended on her to lead them through the rocky maze before them. She knew this path well, having traveled it many times. The Strait ahead was known as the *tail of the snake* after the whipping, churning waters. Tumbling over the semi-buried rocks broken away from the cliffs on either side, a ship could be stranded with one wrong turn. Beyond it was the *curves.*

A challenge for even the strongest captain, she could almost guide her ship safely through these waters with her eyes closed. Every rock and shell was as familiar to her as the stars in the northern sky. Ariana's fingers gripped the wheel tighter as the ship slowly made its way through the narrow gorge. Beneath her feet the deck shuddered slightly as it made its way down the last of the shallow channel and moved into deeper water.

The maze was done and once again they were on the open sea. A full moon loomed before her, the only other thing awake. Its light shining on the still water drew the ship forward at this time of night. Midnight hour. Witching hour. A time when the portal between the here and now stretched into the Otherworld. Ariana's heart raced as if mere wishing would make those sails quicken the journey. At last, they were homeward bound and soon would be in the arms of their families. All that stood between her daughter and Ariana was the moon.

The familiar waters of her hidden cove finally came into view. Midnight hour was almost gone, and she must pass through before the portal closed. Ariana had grown up on tales of her father's secret discovery of the link between Lunadar and the world beyond the moon. How, with each full moon, the portal opened long enough to bridge the two worlds. But the gods were not merciful to those who failed to return through the portal in time. To linger in the Otherworld beyond the full moon would close the portal forever and damn her to life without her daughter, Candra.

The bow parted the still waters, the soft foam riding the gentle wake towards land. She quickly dropped anchor just beyond the shoreline as the portal faded away. Another successful run and a full bounty to share with others. Lord Shemar might have a price on Princess Ariana's head, but the gods favored her tonight. It took some time to ferry everything to shore but eventually the hold was empty. Ariana could finally kneel to bless the ground beneath her feet. She was home and eager to hold Candra in her arms once again.

Leaving the men to load the cargo on wagons bound for Lunadar, Ariana hurried over the cobblestone path leading away from the water's edge. Waiting for her was her faithful stallion, Aramid. Easing into the saddle, she turned his head toward Lunadar and nudged him forward. The steady rhythm of Aramid's hooves striking stone almost lulled her to sleep, but she couldn't rest until she was reassured Candra was safe. It had been three years since Ariana touched her father's face after the Battle of Roth. Three years since Candra's birth and Ariana shouldered the heavy cloak of responsibility for the people of Lunadar. She swore she would make Lord Shemar pay for what he had done to her family. It seemed like only yesterday she played at her father's knee as he ran battle worn fingers through Ariana's long, jet black hair. A lone streak of white snaked its way through the tresses until it ended just short of her waist.

"Mystic hair. It is the source of all your power, child," he would chant to Ariana but never quite answered her questions as to what he meant. "Have patience, little one, you will learn soon enough of your mystic gift of controlling the elements," he would say until she began to feel a whisper of something stirring deep inside her. The taller she grew, the deeper the stirring became, and she began to believe her father might be right. She would gladly cut off that hair now if it could give her one more hour with him. Now, she wore it to honor him and waited for the time when she would get her revenge.

It was a short ride to the castle grounds, and the sounds of the waterfalls grew louder as Ariana entered the courtyard. Built among several waterfalls surrounding it, the castle stood near the cliffs protecting the people of Lunadar from invaders. King Midar chose well to bring his people to this land.

A tall stone wall encircled the grounds and offered added protection. The interior was dark, shadowing the many corridors snaking through the castle; each one offering special access to the waterfalls surrounding it. Ariana's faithful servant, Macklebee, knew of her impending return and had left torches burning to light her way. Stopping only long enough to wake a stable hand to tend to her horse, Ariana wearily climbed the steps leading into the castle and slipped into the kitchen unnoticed by the dozing guard. She would reprimand him later, but for now all she sought was the knowledge Candra slept peacefully before she called upon Breana, guardian of dreams, to release her from today's troubles. Ariana got as far as the washbasin when a pair of tiny arms wrapped themselves around her leg. Looking down, she scooped the sleepy-eyed child into her arms before turning her attention to the servant stepping into the room to stand in front of her.

"Why is my daughter up so late, Macklebee?"

"I am sorry, Princess Ariana, but she heard your horse arrive and would not remain in her chambers without crying for her mama."

Ariana drew Candra closer to her to breathe in the smell of lilacs and sweet water still lingering from her evening bath. If Ariana were a simple woman from the village, her life would be vastly different. Her child would not yearn for a mother lost to the sea. But Ariana was of noble blood, and her life was not of her own choosing. Lord Shemar made sure of that. Now she only prayed there would come a day when she did not have to leave her daughter the next time the full moon rose. There would come a time, hopefully soon, when she would extract her vengeance on her father's murderer, so she could return to Lunadar once and for all.

CHAPTER TWO

Hours later, those same waterfalls greeted her when Ariana woke up. For a moment she forgot where she was, muscles tense against the unfamiliar softness beneath her. Survival depended on anticipating danger and fingers reached for the dirk lying on the table next to her. Her heartbeat slowed as Candra skipped into the room.

Candra had her mother's mystic hair and her grandfather's eyes. The same solitary white strand curled around small fingers while those eyes sparkled at Ariana as she climbed onto the bed. They played for a few minutes before Ariana motioned for her maid to step forward. As much as she would like to have spent the morning in bed with her child, her people were waiting for her to settle their grievances.

Dropping a kiss on Candra's cheek before shooing her back toward the nursery, Ariana allowed her maid to imprison her in a breath-stealing corset and gather her hair into a bun at her nape. Gathering a somber composure about her she didn't fully feel, Ariana descended the staircase and headed toward the great hall. If only she could wear the breeches and short tunic as when she was on her ship, her hair tangled by the wind and not straining against the clips barely holding it in place. Irritation quickly turned to heightened alertness when she stepped into the hallway. Tension hovered in the air and she could almost smell the fear emanating from her people. Walking over to the dais, she quickly sat down and turned to Alasdair, the captain of her troops.

"Alasdair, what has happened?"

He gave a quick glance to where the villagers were gathered before moving to her side to whisper, "It's the Drundles, milady. They have attacked south of Tumac Mountain, and your people irrationally fear Lunadar will be next."

Drundles.

How she loathed the mere mention of their name. For years they had attacked the poor people who lived outside Lunadar's waterfall city, but people behind the fortress walls had little to fear. Her father had chosen the site of his city carefully.

The waterfalls and city walls would deter any Drundles foolish enough to attempt to plunder there. The thick, stone walls were nearly impenetrable, and the Drundle's fear of the water kept them from attempting to breach the castle walls. Yet, she hated the thought of them so near because it reminded her of her unfinished business with Lord Shemar. Half devil, half wildebeest, the Drundles were loyal only to the dark lord, and their poisonous barbs were known to kill a man in less time than it took to blink in surprise at the fact he was struck.

Surely the Drundles were not so foolish as to travel this far south, especially not so close to the Winter's Solstice. All the realms would be represented, far outnumbering the dark lord's assassins.

"Alasdair take your troops and scout to the edge of Tumac Mountain. Bring me back word of where the Drundles are hiding!"

"Right away, milady. I am yours to command."

Her captain strode from the room. Turning her attention to the villagers standing in front of her, fearful eyes stared back at her. They believed in her father's oath of protection. Now she must give them some hope all were as safe within these walls as when her father was alive.

Standing tall with shoulders back, she raised her hand and almost instantly silence filled the great hall. What could she say to those who stood before her? For the past three years they had struggled to carry on after her father's passing. Years of being forced to wait for returned trips from the Otherworld while body and soul struggled to remain together for a little longer. Lord Shemar had reduced Lunadar to this. Her father had often told her stories of them growing up together. Young nobles hell bent on changing the world.

But it was Shemar who changed first and not for the better. Soon, Ariana's father couldn't even recognize the childhood friend in the stony-faced man threatening to destroy him and his beloved Lunadar for the crime of loving the same woman.

Since then, Ariana's father had fought for a future without oppression from the dark lord and his minions, but what had it gained him? A cold, damp grave and an orphaned daughter almost too young to step into her father's shoes. How many times had she wondered if it wouldn't be easier to surrender? To open the doors of Lunadar to Lord Shemar, praying he would be merciful after all they have suffered at his hands. She only had to look into the eyes of her people to realize it would be foolishness to harbor such thoughts. This irrational quest for revenge had poisoned the dark lord's heart and the only treasure he sought was her blood. To think otherwise was to place her people in the gravest of danger.

From the corner of the room a flash of color made its way into the great hall. Candra, free once again from Macklebee's watchful eye, had wandered into the room. She was beloved by the people of Lunadar and the crowd parted like a great sea to let her pass by them. Just as Candra ran to Ariana's side, she knew what she would tell her people. Scooping up Candra into her arms, Ariana plants a kiss upon her hair before turning her attention to the crowd.

"People of Lunadar, please hear me. There was a time when my father ruled this city with great wisdom. A time when your own children were free to go to nearby Dreydan's Falls without fear of what might happen. A time when Lord Shemar could not harm us. I know of your heartache since my father's murder at the Battle of Roth. I hear your cries of anguish when a Drundle's barb takes the life of yet another loved one.

But take heart, dear citizens of Lunadar. The fight is not over yet, and there *will* come a day when our city returns to its former glory! I know this to be true because I can see it in my daughter's eyes. Our children are the future and surely the gods will not let the dark one win. I will fight with all my strength to protect my father's legacy. The Drundles fear the pure waters of the falls. Those same waters and our walls have stood against our foes in the past and will again if the need arises."

She would do anything to protect hearth and home. So would the people of Lunadar. Her resolve to defeat Lord Shemar returned as the crowd cheered for their leader. She breathed a little easier as she turned to the more immediate concern of settling disputes between friend and neighbor. At least she could show the people of Lunadar she was still their leader and protector while she remained at home. But all too soon she would have to make another journey for supplies and a part of her worried about what might happen while she was away?

The sun was high in the sky by the time she finished her duties in the great hall. She often wondered if her father could have done better by the people who stand before her expecting judgement and fairness from their leader. She feared she had failed Lunadar by allowing the uncertainty of their future to leech the very life out of this once great city.

Dismissing the crowd, Ariana crossed the room to gaze at the rushing water tumbling beneath the tower windows. Most of her life she had been lulled by the sound of the waterfalls. They surrounded her city and served as a natural barrier against their enemies. Waves crashing against the rocks and mist rising above the ocean's tide usually calmed her, but not today. News of the Drundles attacking so close to Lunadar did not sit well. A restlessness was building inside her, and only one thing would help ease her worries.

Heading to the stable, Aramid was quickly saddled by a young stable hand, and she rode outside the city's protective walls toward Dreydan's Falls. How wise of King Midar to build on this land. No Drundle dared come near the city if the waters flowed. They may be animals, but even they knew the waterfalls would burn their flesh like acid while their death would be a slow and agonizing one.

She made it to the base of the falls and dismounted to let Aramid drink while she bent down to sip the cooling waters herself. Her fingers made a trail through the ripples before cupping her hands to splash water against her heated brow. Maybe it was the quiet of the surroundings which dulled her senses, but suddenly she was aware of another presence, making the hair on the back of her neck stand on end.

Muscles instantly tensed for fight or flight as she slowly turned to gaze up at Lord Shemar from her still crouched position. The years since her father's death had not softened his features. The coldness in his heart drained the warmth from his eyes, turning them dark grey and glittering with loathing as he stared down the bridge of his nose at her. The rough ridge of a long scar ran up one cheek before disappearing into his hairline. It only served to sharpen his features into a hawkish look as one corner of his mouth curled into a tight smile as he casually glanced around, realizing no guards accompanied her.

Ariana felt her stomach muscles tighten as she watched him slowly move his grey stallion in her direction. How eagerly she'd like to plunge her dagger deep into Lord Shemar's heart, but she was outnumbered by dozens of Drundles standing between her and Aramid. Poisonous barb tips quivered all along their backs as they awaited Lord Shemar's command to attack. Seconds away from a sudden death by one touch of those barbs, Ariana still hesitated attempting to flee.

Slowly rising to stand in front of the dark lord, she could see the hatred in Lord Shemar's eyes as he stared at her in contempt. Her nemesis tugged the reins to still his agitated mount. Even the slight bow from his saddle he gave her was seeped in disrespect before he looked around as if in search of someone.

"So, Lady Ariana, we meet again. And where, pray tell, are your guards? Surely the leader of Lunadar would not be so foolish as to travel outside the gates without some sort of protection?"

Ariana lifted her chin just a tad higher, and not just because Lord Shemar loomed over her. His disrespect at not calling her by her correct title struck a nerve and tightened her mouth. Clenching her fists at her side to steady herself, she glanced at him in what she hoped was a condescending manner and replied, "What need have I of protection in my own kingdom? Are people still not free to roam these lands as they wish? At least they were in King Midar's day."

At the mention of the king's name, Lord Shemar jerked on the reins causing his stallion to quickly sidestep in Ariana's direction. Ariana stepped backwards toward the edge of the waterfall as she heard Lord Shemar hiss, "You dare speak that devil's name in my presence? You were foolish to lower your guard against the vengeance I promised one day to deliver to your door. Now you will follow your father into the bowels of hell by my hand!"

Ariana hoped there was no fear in her eyes as she stared into those dead eyes looking back at her.

"You are sadly mistaken, milord, if you think my father's spirit resides in Hades. Only evil such as yourself will find a home there!"

Ariana knew her words hit its intended mark as the stallion reared in protest to the sharp pull on its reins as Lord Shemar turned away from Ariana, summoning the Drundles to attack.

Whistling sharply to Aramid, Ariana dove headfirst into the middle of the falls. Breaking the surface a few yards away, she felt her horse gather beneath her as they plunged through the waters with the screeching of the Drundles ringing in her ears. A Drundle foolish enough to get too close to it was soon reminded the waters would burn their skin like acid and neutralize their poisonous barbs. They couldn't risk following her into the river but instead raced alongside to narrow the distance between them.

Puffs of steam rose from behind her, the river dissolving the barbs as soon as they landed. She was relatively safe if she remained in the water but would eventually have to cross land to return to the protective walls of Lunadar. Now was not the time to castigate herself for her foolishness in venturing outside the city walls alone. She could only pray there would be time for that later.

Ariana smelled the stench of death drifting closer as the Drundles continued to shorten the distance between them. As much as they feared the water, they hated

Ariana more. To be free of them, she would need to take her chances over land to outrun those poisonous barbs.

But Ariana was not so eager to die today and instead turned Aramid away from Lunadar. She would follow the river to Quallan Forest to seek the protection of Queen Elysie and the creatures who lived there. While Ariana didn't exactly trust the Fairie queen, she seemed loyal to her father once, and Ariana could only hope she remained loyal to his memory.

Ariana heard whispers of Queen Elysie despising Lord Shemar for her own secret reasons, and she hoped this would help sway the queen's decision to offer her the sanctuary of the forest. The sharp hiss of a poisonous barb whizzing by Aramid's head, stabbing the muddy bank just inches away from her, brought Ariana back to the present danger in an instant. Jerking the reins sharply to the left, she crouched lower over the saddle as she urged the stallion on to greater speed. The drumming beat of hooves striking river rock blended with whistling barbs and splashing spray as Ariana raced for the stand of trees rising on the horizon.

The edge of Quallan Forest was just ahead, and she nudged her exhausted mount forward. She couldn't allow Aramid to stop now. The sound of the Drundles were fading into the distance, and she could barely hear the frustration in their screeches as they realized their prize was about to get away. Drundles would not dare enter Quallan Forest without Queen Elysie's permission as only she could ensure their safe travel through the water filled forest.

A sweat-drenched Aramid weaved his way through the edge of the forest as the trees seemed to entwine their branches behind him. There would be no returning to Dreydan's Falls the way they had come. She would soon find out her fate as she headed toward the green glowing lights of Quallan Castle, tucked away in the middle of the forest. Ariana's only hope of survival was to pray the queen was in a forgiving mood.

CHAPTER THREE

Aramid had ceased to blow, the sweat drying on his coat in the cool air of the forest. His reins hung loosely in Ariana's hands, her companion content to keep pace with her as she led him down the path between the huge trees surrounding them. They had not gone far when the soft sound of fairy wings began to drum the air all around her. She couldn't see them, except for the occasional flicker in her peripheral vision, but the rustling of the branches above her announced the creatures of Quallan Forest were hiding in nervous anticipation.

Fairie mothers gathered their babies close to them, clicking in some unknown language to silence their chatter. Soldier fairies hovered behind tree trunks, their wings drumming a soft cadence as they stole glances at the intruder below. Queen Elysie guarded her people well and they in turn were loyal to her. Not one step could Ariana take without watchful eyes following her every move. She knew the danger involved for entering unannounced, and yet the forest creatures simply watched her as she passed by. The cloyingly sweet smell of fear hung in the air because she was strange to them. They knew she was from Lunadar. They would know also of her hate for Lord Shemar, and Ariana could almost read their minds. What evil lurked beyond those woven branches they might wonder?

Slowly at first, then faster, rays of sunshine filtered through the treetops, shimmering and swirling until it began to materialize into a form in front of Ariana. The Fairie queen's unexpected appearance startled Ariana and even the trees were stilled by her silent arrival. Queen Elysie's emerald gown almost blended into the lush green carpet of the forest floor. Blue-green wings that matched her eyes stretched out on either side of her, gently disturbing the glittering sunshine with each fluttering beat of wingtips.

Few outside the Fae world had ever seen her up close other than at the annual Winter Solstice celebration. *Why was the queen herself here instead of one of her guards?* Ariana wondered. Sweat beaded along her brow and the hair stuck to her neck as she bowed before one older than time. She recalled all the tales her father told her about Queen Elysie and Quallan Forest. Ariana was no match for one powerful like the Fairie queen. Ariana stared at the ground and waited for her to speak.

"Why have you come here?"

A voice somewhere between a dove's sigh and a serpent's hiss sent shivers down Ariana's spine as she bowed lower still, "I beg for your mercy. The Drundles seek my blood, and I might not return to Lunadar safely without your help."

"And why should I help you, daughter of King Midar? My loyalty was to your father, not to his heir."

"It's because of him I seek your help. I know of his loyalty to you and your people. And you know it was Lord Shemar who took my father from Lunadar. We have the same enemy and we both thirst for revenge for the dark lord threatens both our kingdoms." She held her breath and clenched her clammy hands to calm them. Had she said the right words to gain the queen's mercy? All around the forest twittered nervously.

Queen Elysie muttered a few words in an ancient tongue, and Aramid was spirited away by a troop of soldier fairies. Ariana waited in silence, hoping Aramid would be okay but too nervous to ask the queen where he was being taken. One word crackled into the silence and relief washed over her like a spring rain.

"Come!"

Queen Elysie quickly glided through the forest. Ariana raced to keep up. Fairie lights twinkled among the trees and the forest waters glowed green. The queen seemed to glide along the forest floor. Creatures cleared a path and trees bowed as she passed by. Ariana was being led further away from Quallan Castle and deeper into the forest. She could only place her trust in the hands of those she did not trust while allowing the shadows to surround her. She barely made out the image slowly growing before her as they neared what appeared to be some sort of land portal hidden deep within the shadows of the trees.

As they approached the edge of the steps leading to a door with a crescent carved into its surface, Queen Elysie turned to Ariana. This time, Ariana heard a soft, musical voice full of longing say,

"Your father was a strong ruler; a just leader who fought for the safety of all under his protection. There was truth in your words, daughter of King Midar. We do share the same enemy, yet for very different reasons. Yours because Lord Shemar sees in you the obstacle to his becoming leader of Lunadar so he can erase your father's memory. Mine because he took something most precious from me even as your father tried to guard it. For this alone I will do as you ask and show you the secret passage I have guarded for centuries."

"Before you is a land portal between Quallan Forest and Lunadar. Your father used it at times when it was unsafe for his troops to return home by way of the falls. The day King Midar perished at the Battle of Roth was the day I swore to one day repay your father's loyalty to my kingdom. Return to Lunadar in safety and live to fight another day. My debt to your father's loyalty has now been paid."

Ariana didn't even know how to begin to thank the Fairie queen. All those years and her father never told her of this land portal. Never told her the reason for the bond between him and the leader of Quallan Forest. What other secrets had her own father kept from her?

Before she could speak, the queen disappeared into a gathering mist and Ariana was left alone except for a slight breeze rustling the tree branches above her head. She hoped Aramid had been treated as kindly as herself. Straightening her shoulders and sending a prayer of thanks to the gods, she reached for the ornate knob on the portal door. Slowly opening it, Ariana could just make out the waterfalls of Lunadar beyond the fog clouding her view.

It felt almost like she was stepping into a slippery bog, and she closed her eyes for a moment. Some unknown force was dragging her down and she felt powerless to fight it. Just when Ariana thought she would suffocate beneath the heavy, oppressive feeling pressing down on her, she found herself outside the gates of Lunadar with the late afternoon sun peeking through the trees. Aramid waited for her there, well fed and rested during her audience with Queen Elysie.

There was much to prepare for in the coming days, and Ariana would never again lower her guard while Lord Shemar and the Drundles lurked outside the gates. Lunadar's supplies would only last for so long. All too soon she must leave Candra again and return to the sea.

Ariana pushed her thoughts concerning her father's loyalty to Quallan Forest to the back of her mind as she entered the castle grounds. Alasdair had returned and judging by his fierce frown, the news he had to bear was unwelcome.

Alasdair lowered to one knee before speaking, "We discovered many dead, milady, but did what we could for those left behind who were in need of supplies."

Worry still lingered in his face he could not hide from her. Narrowing her eyes as she continued to stare at her captain Ariana said, "Come, Alasdair, do not hide your concerns from me. I grew up in your shadow and know your every thought almost before you do. Tell me what other worry colors your eyes so?"

"In truth, my princess, it is the festival which troubles me more than the Drundles."

She was momentarily surprised. The Winter Solstice celebration? "Why does this cause you such concern?"

The man before her visibly struggled to find the words.

"Prince Kaspar will be attending the celebration," he finally said in hushed tones.

Her stomach lurched. She had tried to erase that name from her memory ever since she discovered she was with child. For a moment the floor beneath her feet seemingly shifted. Only sheer will power kept her rooted to her spot. She struggled to keep an iron grip on her treacherous mind as it replayed a winter solstice dance before her father's death tore her world apart.

Her father was preparing for the Battle of Roth and the impending victory over Lord Shemar but delayed his troops departure, so they might participate in the annual festivities before facing the grim reality of battle. Ariana felt so ignorant of the world back then, barely past her fourteenth year, and looking forward to the mermaids' dance in honor of her father. Queen Naab, ruler of all creatures living beneath the ocean was to attend as well as her son, Prince Kaspar.

Ariana had never met the prince but had heard certain tales of this tantalizing merman. Back then she was just as certain she would never fall for his charms. Oh, how naive she had been. How gullible to think a creature of the sea would not be ruled by the moon, and how easily she misjudged her own sensibilities in the ways of the heart.

What's done was done and no amount of gnashing of teeth would change the events. All of Lunadar knew only another mermaid would be a suitable mate for the heir to Renndar. A mystic and a merman may fall in love, but where would their true allegiance lie? For this reason alone, Queen Naab forbade such a union, but by then it was too late to prevent a legacy from being born.

On winter solstice eve, sea creatures could walk upon the land, and Ariana never realized who Prince Kaspar was until it was too late. The costumes worn for the fairy's dance hid well his face from her. Even so, Ariana should have seen through the mask. Should have paid more attention to the warnings whispered about the binding magic to be found within the haunting mermaid melody when heard while in the moon's shadow. She should have known better than to allow his silken words to tempt her, but moon melting into mermaid's song were to become her downfall that night.

As the first few notes coiled around her, snaking its way into her senses, Ariana felt helplessly trapped by the glow coming from those deep green pools staring back at her from behind the mask. It wasn't until later when Prince Kaspar returned to the sea that she discovered who danced with her under the shadow of moonlight.

Oh, how the taste of deceit was bitter upon her tongue. It was then she swore she would never reveal the father of her child's identity. Only Alasdair and Macklebee knew of her secret, and it would go to their graves, of that she was certain.

Not only must she worry about the dark lord and his minions sweeping ever closer to Lunadar's gates, but must she now also steel mind and body against treachery from her own heart? It was well known how the undersea queen felt about land dwellers. A century-long tradition was the only reason the queen still attended the winter festivities.

Civility must be maintained for the sake of an uneasy peace, but Ariana knew what would happen if Candra's lineage was ever uncovered. She had managed so far to hide her secret within the walls of the castle. But Ariana knew her own blood would flow like the waterfalls before she endangered her daughter's life by letting her become

some pawn in a battle between the ocean realm of
Renndar and Lunadar!

25

CHAPTER FOUR

The next few weeks flew by. Everywhere around her, preparations for the winter's solstice celebration were underway, and eager anticipation lit up the faces of her people. The shortest night of the winter would soon be upon them, and all would gather to feast. The people living within the walls of Lunadar gathered fresh holly berry and greenery to decorate the great hall.

Those living outside the walls but under its protection chose what they could to honor a fallen king and the daughter who led them now. All around, spirits were lifted at the thought that for at least one night there would be enough to fill bellies and a reason to dance. Even Lord Shemar and the Drundles were forgotten. There was strength in numbers. Who would dare to attack Lunadar when all are gathered within its walls?

Finally, winter solstice was here. One last feast before Ariana and her men must travel through the portal once more in search of supplies. Ariana's table sat on a small dais along one wall and oversaw the trestle tables filling the rest of the room.

Two hundred would celebrate this night as moon, ocean, and forest gather together as one. In times past, she would watch as her father gave the toast to bless his people and pray to the gods for another peaceful year.

This night she must lead the people in a prayer lying heavily upon her heart. She would pray the gods be merciful and end the evil darkening their happiness. May this year be the time when she had her revenge upon Lord Shemar and finally drive the Drundles from Lunadar forever. She wished with all her heart the return of peace to the land so her own child might have the freedom to visit Dreydan's Falls as Princess Ariana did in her own youth.

Servants were arranging candles about the room as she strode between the tables on her way to her chambers. She had ordered extra lights this night as she wished her guests to feel the warmth of a bright new future was still within their grasp. All that was left was to make sure Candra would be kept safely hidden in the nursery during the festivities before preparing for her role as hostess and ruler of Lunadar.

Her daughter's laughter rang through the corridor as she approached the nursery. After opening the door, she saw Macklebee entertaining Candra on the floor with a funny dance by her poppet doll.

"It pleases me to see my daughter delights in your antics, Macklebee."

Her manservant rose quickly to his feet, a pink flush staining his cheeks, as he held the toy behind him. "We did not hear you come in, milady."

"No harm done. I have come to visit Candra before I must ready myself for tonight's festivities." She scooped her daughter into her arms. Tiny fingers wrapped themselves around her waist long hair. Candra was fascinated with its length. Her child was half mermaid, half mystic and Ariana wondered just how much Candra was beginning to understand the nature of her mother's mystic heritage, much less her father's.

Even Ariana did not know if she inherited the power of the ocean; to breathe underwater and command creatures of the sea. Such a discovery involved being reborn to the ocean and it was a risk Ariana could not fathom taking just to learn the truth. Far better to live in ignorance of a potential legacy gift given to her daughter. Besides, what need did she have of such a gift? Candra was destined to become ruler of Lunadar one day and Ariana firmly believed a mother's gift of controlling earth and sky would protect her far more than any other power might.

She halted her daydreaming when she heard Macklebee giving instructions to the maid regarding Candra's evening meal. After kissing her on the tip of her nose and inhaling the sweet scent of lavender, Ariana handed her daughter to her nurse and turned to Macklebee,

"Everything is secure for tonight, Macklebee?"

"Yes, milady. Alasdair has increased the guards throughout the castle and sentries are posted all along the outer wall. Your people will be able to enjoy the festivities without worry."

"And my daughter?"

"She will remain in the nursery per your command. Neither Queen Naab nor her son shall discover her identity this night. Even now she prepares for sleep and can barely keep her eyes open."

Ariana glanced over to see her daughter's eyes half closed, head drooping as she tried to eat the porridge her nanny was feeding her. Ariana shuddered to think what would happen should the ruler of the ocean discover Candra.

The child might look like her mother, but the sea queen would be able to see past those looks with questions too dangerous to answer. If Queen Naab ever figured out the child was born of a union between her son and Ariana, she would see it as an act of war; an attempt to interfere with the succession in her kingdom. The older Candra got, the harder it became to keep the secret hidden within the walls of Lunadar.

Two hours soon passed as maids bathed her, dried her hair and clothed her in layers of silk. Tonight, Ariana wore a silver-white gown that shimmered as the moonlight danced off diamonds sewn into the cloth.

More diamonds were woven into her upswept hair until she looked like she was born of the mist curling outside the castle door.

She gazed at herself in the mirror and saw wide, dark eyes staring back at her. Her knees were shaking slightly, and her palms grew sweaty. She gave herself a mental shake and clenched her fists to stop their trembling. She had a feeling Prince Kaspar would seek her out tonight and she was not sure of her ability to resist his charms.

Older and wiser now, she was not so foolish as she was in her youth, but she had yet to shake his spell over her. The past two festivals he did not attend. Rumors spread like wildfire as to the reason for his absence, but Ariana knew. Now she heard he would come tonight. She must steel mind and body against his ways. Once caught by the mermaid's song, forever trapped until the dawn the legend went and she feared she was not strong enough to resist his song should Prince Kaspar choose to come for her tonight.

Drawing a deep breath to steady nerves, she strode regally to the great hall. The aroma of roasting mutton and pork filled the air. Tables strained under the weight of platters filled with fresh fruit, cheeses, and desserts. Laughter mingled with the sound of eating as all Lunadar enjoyed bowl shaped bread trenchers filled with seal stew. Her people did not usually dine so well these days, and tonight children would sleep with full bellies.

Her own stomach muscles tightened as she neared her chair. Already she felt the low hum of the mermaid's call curling around low in the pit of her stomach. It was as if his spirit reached out to hers and the battle of wills began even before she sat down. Alasdair hovered near her side and she waved him away.

She sailed the high seas and always brought home enough food to help feed her people until the next voyage was needed. She had battled Lord Shemar and his Drundles. Can she not handle one merman?

Queen Elysie was to Ariana's left, a place of honor, while her high priestess Tomari was next to her. On Ariana's right was Queen Naab, while Prince Kaspar occupied the seat next to her. During other solstice celebrations, Ariana sat opposite her father at this very table, back when the people of Lunadar were happy, enemies were few, and the moon was the bond holding them together. Now the years of fighting had planted seeds of mistrust. Who at this table would come to her aid in her fight to save Lunadar should she ever need them?

She made small talk with Queen Elysie and Tamari about the growing threat of the Drundles. She even managed to entice Queen Naab to regale them with tales of past adventures with King Midar. To Prince Kaspar she said little beyond what was demanded. Distance was her weapon, avoidance her shield, against the pull she felt all night. Tension was building inside her and by the time the fairies had performed their dance to honor her father's memory, the air in the great hall had become too stifling for her to bear.

Ariana left her guests to their merriment and made her way to the mezzanine. All Lunadar had waited for this night and now how she wished it were over. If only the morning sun would be waiting outside the castle windows to greet her.

She stopped before the portrait of her father. King of Lunadar. How could she imagine she could ever take his place? The weight of responsibility and this never-ending war with the dark lord was taking its toll on her. It was barely the eighteenth year of her birth and already she felt as old as the Fairie queen. Her father's portrait blurred as she wiped her eyes.

It was then she felt his presence.

Prince Kaspar stepped from the shadows not far from her. The rhythm of his song inside her pulsated so strongly, she didn't even stop to wonder why the prince was in this part of the castle. She struggled to rein in her tears, a loss for words stilling her tongue.

"Why the tears, Princess Ariana?"

She should have known she could not avoid that merman forever. She reminded herself of his treacherous deceit to still her heart's rampant beating. She told herself it didn't matter he had grown more handsome in the years since she last saw him. Taking a steady breath, she turned to face her past.

"Why are you here, Prince Kaspar?"

"You didn't answer my question."

"It's none of your concern. A mere whisper of a past memory is all."

Kaspar said nothing for a moment, simply stared at Ariana until she began to feel a flush heat up her cheeks, and she turned to look at her father's portrait once again.

"Oh, I wager it is more than a fleeting memory to cause such strong emotion in one such as yourself."

Harsh words pushed past sudden tears threatening to spill again as Ariana whirled to face the merman. "How dare you presume to know me! You know nothing about me!"

Sea green eyes turned almost smoky as Kaspar slowly studied Ariana. His voice, roughened by something Ariana couldn't understand, cut across the distance between them. "Oh, milady, I believe I know you much more intimately than you may acknowledge, but know you, I do!"

They danced with words, Prince Kaspar and Ariana, in the corridor. For every verbal step he advanced, she retreated. There was a smile tugging at his lips she wished she could wipe from his face. He thought he knew her. But Ariana knew he would fail at this game because he was as fickle as the tide, and his song could not last forever.

She turned her back on him in disdain and looked again at her father's face. Such strength. Such wisdom and compassion. There was a saying, if wishes were horses all beggars would ride. How she wished at this very moment she was upon Aramid's back and far from this place. Tendrils of hair moved aside by the prince's breath tickling her shoulder as Prince Kaspar stepped closer to her. Tension coiled even tighter within her, making her thrust her shoulders back and clench her fists to her side.

"Do you weep for your father, milady? He was a wise and kind leader. Lunadar lost a great king that day at the Battle of Roth. But the king's daughter stays true to his legacy and is also a strong leader of her people."

The words slid across her skin and she closed her eyes for a moment. How long will she be able to fight this spell he had over her? His song was whispering to her again and her spirit cried out to follow him, but she must remember it was nothing but mist and moonlight. There was no place for her in his world, nor he in hers, and to think otherwise would be sheer madness.

She turned to face the prince. Her quick movement momentarily surprised him, and he stepped back a pace, just enough for her to catch her breath and gather her thoughts. The only way to win this battle between them was to strike the first blow.

"Why have you come here? You are not welcome!

CHAPTER FIVE

Prince Kaspar gazed at her with those sea green eyes of his for a moment before replying, "I did not come tonight to cause you distress, Princess Ariana. In truth, I came tonight because I cannot stay away any longer. You may have forgotten what it was like between us the last time I visited Lunadar, but I have not. I wonder if you are not part witch as well as mystic for I am enchanted to return to your side."

Driven by a need to protect Candra and maybe even her own treacherous heart, Ariana lashed out at the merman, "I was a mere child back then and you were a full-grown man when we first met. You knew better than to seduce me, in my own home, while under my father's protection! Do you think me such a fool? I know you for who you really are! A creature of the water who merely entices others to their doom with your mermaid song. Sea sorcerer who preys upon the innocence of young girls and promises them the treasures of the deep, only to dash their hopes upon the rocks with the break of dawn!"

Ariana saw those sea green eyes darken like an incoming storm as he grabbed her arms and pulled her closer to him. She watched in nervous fascination as his jaw muscles clinched tighter as his breath was harsh upon her lips.

"Is that what you really think of me? How was I to know the creature I stumbled upon that night in the moonlight was the king's daughter? You never gave me your name, no matter how many times I asked, and you teased my senses until I thought I would go mad if I didn't make you mine. And afterwards, you were gone like the mist without a word!"

She pulled herself from his grasp, her own eyes narrowing as she said, "As if you weren't privy to your own mother's feelings about land dwellers. I had heard about your trickery with females before, but I didn't know just how far you would go to deceive an innocent!"

For a moment she thought she saw a flash of surprise cross the prince's face, only to be replaced by a growing look of confusion. Confusion not directed at her but at something behind her. Ariana turned to look at what captured his attention and felt her heart skip a beat. Running toward her and calling for her mama was Candra. Somehow Ariana's daughter had once again escaped the watchful eye of Macklebee at the worst possible moment and was running straight into danger!

Prince Kaspar took a step forward as if to go toward the child as Ariana put one hand out in front of her and quickly pulled Candra to her side to shield her from his view as much as possible. She saw her manservant rushing down the hall toward them and knew in that instant her world would never be the same. She turned to face Prince Kaspar as he looked first at Candra, then Macklebee, before looking at Ariana with eyes as black as the ocean floor.

"Who is this child?"

For a moment she thought to tell him anything but the truth. To say anything but the words that would begin the battle for her daughter's life. But she couldn't. She couldn't hide from the truth now. Standing taller, she lifted her chin and said, "She is my daughter."

"And who is her father?"

Ariana could not bring herself to say the words and her silence only served to infuriate the merman more. His fists clinched at his side to match her own as he thrusted his face toward hers, saying, "Do you take me for a fool, Princess Ariana? Even a simpleton could do the sums and see this child is the right age to be mine! Who is the deceitful one now? Unless you think to tell me false tales of some other lover who came to you on that same Winter Solstice eve?"

"Who Candra's father is should be of no concern to you. She is my daughter and future ruler of Lunadar and that is all you need know!"

They stood there like two raging beasts, bent on defeating each other, when suddenly Candra began to cry in fear from the tension she could feel emanating from Ariana and Prince Kaspar.

As Ariana picked Candra up to calm her, she could see the merman in front of her struggle to calm his rage. It did no good to wage a war here and she motioned for Macklebee to leave them before turning back to Prince Kaspar.

"Is she mermaid or mystic?"

Ariana could see him trying to process this new information he had fathered a child as he watched Candra play with Ariana's hair. How strange it must seem to him. Mother and daughter cut from the same cloth; same mystic hair which now inspired him to ask such a thing.

"I'm not sure."

"What do you mean, you're not sure? Why has she not gone through the water test?"

He sounded incredulous at the possibility, but how could she explain her fear? Her child must drown first to see if the mermaid powers are released and she inherits the ability to live underwater. If not, Candra would be lost to her forever. How could she look into her child's eyes and take that risk? Wasn't being mystic enough?

She tightened her grip on Candra to the point the child began to squirm. Ariana leaned to set her down when the hair on the back of her neck rose at the voice coming from the top of the stairs.

"What is going on here? I thought I heard my son's voice and came to check on him." Queen Naab's words fell into the deafening silence as the sea queen stared first at Ariana, then her son, before settling stormy eyes on the child standing in front of her.

"Whose child is that?"

The day Ariana prayed would never come had arrived. Her instincts told her it would not go well. Ariana was little more than a teenager when the queen warned her away from her son. The confrontation between King Midar and Queen Naab at the time had almost destroyed one of the Winter Solstice celebrations. In the end, the king managed to ease the tension, but the message to Ariana was clear. A mystic wasn't a worthy partner for the prince of the sea.

Queen Naab's face was flush with fury as she approached the small group. It only took one look at the two of them for her to realize Princess Ariana's secret. Her eyes were stormy, dark grey as she glared at her.

"You dared to defy my wishes regarding a union with my son? I told you before you would not have him. And now you think me a fool? Princess Ariana, mark my words. You will regret the day you brought that child into this world!"

As Queen Naab turned to leave, Prince Kaspar glanced once more at his daughter before looking at Ariana to say, "Think well on what you have done, milady. My mother will not stop until my daughter is with the mermaids where she belongs, or at the bottom of the sea. Either way, she will be lost to you forever if the queen has her way!"

With that, he followed his mother out of the castle and into the night. Candra began to cry again as Ariana dropped to her knees to gather her close to her. She could barely control her shaking as she wondered what would happen now. Had she worked so hard these past three years to protect Lunadar's legacy only to lose her now?

As if summoned by the mist, Macklebee returned and helped them both to Ariana's chamber. No words were spoken. None were needed as the damage was already done. No amount of wishing would make it otherwise. Candra was given to her nurse and Macklebee left Ariana to the care of her maids. Alasdair would see to her guests and make any apologies necessary to Queen Elysie and Tomari. The merriment in the great hall would continue for hours, but for Lunadar's leader, the winter's solstice celebration was over.

Soon Ariana must leave Candra again as their supplies were running low. Oh, how she wished she could send someone else in her place, but only she and her men knew where moon and water met to create the portal. She trusted her own ability to see her men safely home from the Otherworld, while thankfully, there was Alasdair and Macklebee to keep her daughter safe while she was away.

She could blame Macklebee for allowing Candra to escape the nursery, but Candra was her mother's daughter and a strong-willed child. Even at so young an age, she had a mind of her own and yearned to run free. She could blame Prince Kaspar for singing his mermaid's song to her. For taking her innocence when he knew his mother's wrath would doom any union from the start. But what good would pointing the finger at someone else do her?

No, the fault was hers for thinking she could hide this secret forever. Now she could only pray the gods would show mercy and allow Candra to remain by her side. Her body was exhausted, but her mind raced as she thought of all that must be done before her ship left with the next high tide. She would get little sleep that night.

CHAPTER SIX

Dawn broke the stillness on the day they pulled away from the harbor. Ariana had no choice but to trust the life of her daughter to Alasdair and her troops. She had informed him of Queen Naab's threat and Candra would remain within the walls of Lunadar to await her return. Candra's cries at Ariana's departure tore at her heart, but already her thoughts were on the task before her.

Some of the men scurried to secure the rigging while others put their backs to setting sail as she turned the bow toward the rising sun. Lunadar was said to be the balancing force between the outer world and what lay beyond the portal. Lunadar's days were its nights and so they must leave by daybreak to reach the moon portal there. The cloak of darkness helped conceal what they must do to survive.

Moonlight shimmered on the water as they left the portal behind and turned westward. The stars guided them while dolphins played in the wake as the ship reached the open sea. Ariana walked the length of the galleon as the men readied the cannons lining the deck. She hated herself for what they had become because of the dark lord. Where was the honor in this? Where was the glory?

To defend hearth and home was one thing, but to take from another without just cause was wrong. *But wasn't saving her people from starving a just cause?* Many a night she laid awake wondering if she had not dammed the people of Lunadar to the punishment of the gods for the chances they took in the Otherworld.

Her leather boots made no sound as she climbed the steps to the quarterdeck. Gone were the cumbersome dresses she was forced to wear in Lunadar. They were replaced with trousers and waistcoat over a white tunic. Her father's dagger rested in her sash and her trusty dirk lay hidden in her boot. The sea breeze lifted her hair as she stood at the wheel and gazed out over the water. Prince Kaspar and the queen must not invade her thoughts today. The risk was high whenever they ventured to this world, and she must plan when a strike would be to their advantage.

They had been sailing for hours and voices were lulled into hushed mumblings by the rhythm of the waves as the men went about their business. Searching the horizon for any sign of movement, Ariana finally saw a set of sails. Muscles tensed as her eyes stared into the distance to make out the owner of this ship. She breathed a sigh of relief as she recognized it as a merchant vessel. It would be no match for them, and she called out to the men below.

"Look alive, men, for our bounty awaits!"

The air fairly crackled with energy as her crew rushed to prepare for the upcoming battle. Voices shouted out across the deck as each man ran to his station. Gunpowder and cannon balls were loaded while weapons were checked once more for readiness. It pleased her that they had yet to have one casualty during the many moons they had been forced to make this run, and she sent a prayer to the gods today would be the same.

As the ship cut through the water, gaining ground against the lumbering merchant ship, Ariana ordered her second in command to make ready the flag which would tell the other captain their intentions were not honorable ones. She wished for the day when she would fly this flag no more, but until then the skull and crossbones under the full moon would continue to lead her men to victory on the seas.

The sudden turn of the other ship told Ariana all she needed to know. The other captain had seen their colors and was trying to make a run for it, but it would be too late to save his cargo. Waves crashed against the merchant ship's bow as the captain desperately tried to distance Itself from Ariana and her crew. His ship's wide, lumbering hull was superior for storing supplies but doomed it to be outrun by Ariana's faster, more streamlined one.

Ariana's men drew their ship within fighting range when she saw the merchant ship's gun begin to fire. What false bravery, admired Ariana, before she gave the order to return fire. The command was always the same. Damage, but do not destroy. Wound if necessary, but never kill. They may be forced into piracy, but they are not without their humanity.

The merchant ship's dozen guns did little to stop them and soon Ariana's ship drew alongside the other ship. Grappling hooks flew as her men swung over the short distance to land onboard the other deck. Steel clashed with steel as the men fought, but Ariana's crew quickly seized control of the vessel. As she prepared to board the other ship, Ariana could see the astonishment the other captain tried to hide from her when he realized the pirate ship was captained by a female.

"What is the meaning of this? How dare you stop my ship!"

His indignation meant nothing to her. Lord Shemar's betrayal forced her actions now and, in her fight to save Lunadar, she could not afford to be swayed by the feelings of outsiders. She saw her men easily outnumbered his and their captives stood defeated as she passed by them to stand before their captain.

"My meaning should be very clear, my dear Captain. I intend to take your cargo."

Indignation turned to anger as his eyes traveled from her trousers back to her eyes before he said, "Your words sound like a noblewoman's, but only a guttersnipe dressed like a pirate would stoop so low as to plunder another man's ship while pretending to be a lady!" Her men's anger matched his at the attack to Ariana's honor, and she acted quickly before any more fighting broke out.

"Forgive me, Captain, if my attire offends you. Corsets and gowns would only hamper my ability to captain my ship, just as wearing them would hamper your own. As for my actions being more suited to that of a pirate than a lady, circumstances force me to do what I must to survive.

Were things any different, you and I would not be having this conversation right now, and my men would be homeward bound. But since this is the fate the gods have given us, pray let us at least be civil to one another and quickly complete the task at hand so we may both be on our way."

Ariana's opponent saw he had no choice but to comply, and she left her men to their work. Cargo was quickly transferred to their ship and after dismantling their cannons to prevent further attack, Ariana set sail for the nearest port still willing to welcome them. Another run finished, and disaster averted. The longer she remained on these seas, the greater the risk they would be caught and hung for piracy. Angry merchant ship owners had created a net slowly closing around them.

Word had spread among the ships at sea to be on the lookout for Lunadar's flag, and there was a heavy bounty for Ariana's capture. If she swung from the gallows for sea crimes, there would be no one to protect Candra, and Lord Shemar would have Lunadar at last. There was a time, not long ago in Lunadar, when she could travel wherever she wished without constantly looking over her shoulder or wondering about a price upon her head. But now she snuck around in the Otherworld like some lowly thief, forever worrying lest some eager captain sought to challenge her freedom.

Life on the sea was a never-ending cycle. Ariana could tell her men were growing tired of these forced trips with nothing but the water and each other to keep them company. Petty disagreements more often flared into heated arguments; more than once she had had to impart some form of discipline to return order to the ship. Her men were loyal to her, but they were still human, and tension could be lived with for just so long before something snapped.

They had sailed those seas for days now and had turned their sails toward Lunadar when she noticed an unknown ship on the horizon heading in their direction. Twilight was fast approaching, and they needed to head for the portal if they were to return to Lunadar in time before it closed. The vessel had the makings of a merchant ship, but something told her this was no lumbering target loaded with silk and spices headed for some distant port.

Their hold was almost full; almost enough to take care of the people of Lunadar for a while but the men urged

Ariana to engage this final target in battle. The harsh winter months lie ahead of them, and this ship would be the difference between a full belly and cries heard in the night from hungry children. It would not take long, and they could return to the portal in plenty of time. Still, she could not shake the uneasy feeling that came over her. She paced the deck while watching the mystery ship inch its way ever closer to them. What if it was another pirate ship seeking to overtake them and steal their much-needed supplies? What if it was a warship commissioned to hunt them down and bring them to justice?

She wished she knew for certain what was really before her. At the urging of her men and against her better judgment, she gave the command to make ready for the fight ahead of them. Maybe she should turn her sails and leave the other captain behind, but the nagging fear of her people starving these next few months pushed her to lay her concerns aside and prepare to lead her men into battle.

CHAPTER SEVEN

Ariana heard the dreaded sound of cannon fire just seconds before the deck was jolted from under her feet. War ship! They had been caught unawares by a dreaded war ship and only now did her colors warn them of her intentions. Racing to the quarterdeck as yet another round of shots was heard, Ariana yelled for her men to return fire.

Grabbing the wheel, she quickly turned the ship about and raced northward. They may still have time to outrun their enemy, but they must also prepare for the possibility Ariana would need to call upon her mystic powers to save the ship and its crew.

She remembered the promise she made to her father never to use her mystic gift to harm another and until today she had been able to keep that promise. Even as he dying on the battlefield, he would not let her vow to unleash the power within and annihilate his enemies.

"My darling daughter, to use your mystic powers come with great risk. You are old enough now to understand that to call upon such power will only drain your own life force until it controls you more than you control it. And how do you know innocents might not die in the process?"

"But father, Lord Shemar has betrayed you!" she wept as she cradled his broken body.

Coughing on the blood slowly oozing from the side of his mouth, her father struggled to reach one last time to touch the strand of white hair as he whispered, "Uphold the legacy of Lunadar, my child, and do not let Shemar's evil consume you."

With that, he was gone, and Ariana's life changed forever. She had struggled many times since that day to honor her father's dying wish. The power within her yearned to be set free, to seek vengeance against Lord Shemar and his Drundles. To make the dark lord pay for the pain he had brought to Lunadar and the evil he had cast upon her people. But dishonoring her father's memory would be to lose him again, and she couldn't bear the shame of such a deed. So, she waited and calmed her spirit with the promise that her time would come, and Lord Shemar would pay for his crimes against her family.

Her mind jerked back to the present as another cannonball struck the ship and the jolt almost tore the wheel from her hands. Her ship was slowly pulling away from the other one, but their long-range cannons still managed to damage the hull and shards from the wooden planks showered down on her men as they struggled to return fire. A small fire broke out on her right but was quickly put out.

Suddenly from above her she heard a thunderous cracking sound as the ship's main mast was struck by a chain-shot, a lucky hit for the enemy captain at this distance, but a calamity for her. Canvas sails crashed to the deck as those below scrambled to get out of harm's way. Her men were near panic, and she could almost feel the captain of the war ship thinking his prize was within reach.

No longer could she stand by to allow her ship and crew to be torn apart piece by piece. Her powers were never meant to be used in her own favor. Her father had made sure of that and her mostly jet-black hair was proof she was still in control of it. It was shortly before her father's death that she learned the link between using mystic powers and the white streak she now wore. Sending a prayer to the gods to protect them, Ariana hoped her father's spirit would forgive her for what she was about to do.

Releasing the wheel, Ariana stepped back a pace and closed her eyes. Calling to the power within her, she repeated the chants of those long gone. She could feel the very air pulsating with unnatural energy. The hair on her arms began to stand on end as she slowly raised them to the heavens.

Black hair, mystic hair, flowed upwards as a mist began to gather around the ship; slowly at first and then as a thick fog forming a wall between their broken vessel and the one pursuing them. Her ship was pushed forward as the waves thickened and rose to heights of twenty feet or more. She knew the crew of the war ship would be fighting to control their vessel as wave after wave slammed into their hull, spinning them off course. Ariana fought to control the uncontrollable.

The sound of Ariana's voice could barely be heard above the roar of the incoming storm. Mere minutes had passed but it seemed like an eternity. Slowly she began to lower her voice to a whisper as her arms returned to her side and she felt the exhaustion beginning to seep into her bones. Her hair, now sporting two white streaks snaking through the ebony, slid back onto her shoulders as the waves returned to normal.

The fog bank began to fade as she opened her eyes and reached for the wheel once more. She didn't need to look around to know the ship was no longer behind them. If its captain was a smart one, he would have turned his ship away from danger before too much damage was done. If not, the creatures of the deep had much to celebrate that night.

Ariana turned her attention back to her ship. The main sail lay in a heap on the deck below her. Pieces of canvas had been torn away when the mast fell, and broken strips of wood was strewn about the deck as her men climbed over the wreckage to access the damage done by the war ship. She had no need to hear from her crew to know things did not bode well for them. She leaned weakly against the railing. There was a price to be paid for calling upon mystic power and she could do nothing now but wait for her strength to slowly return.

They were crippled in the water and only crawled at a slug's pace without their main sail carrying the ship. These waters were treacherous for those who had no choice but to take from others, and they were like sitting ducks against anyone seeking blood justice. Time was running out and the portal might close without them. Ariana could only hope they would make it to the portal in time.

Two hours slowly crawled by, and they had made little progress on their journey. Gone was the main mast, slowing them down with its broken sails and rigging. It was a small price to pay to watch it sink below the waves as the men hoisted most of it over the side if it would guarantee they made it home safely. Her men would not look at her as they went about their work. She would have been able to see their worry over their circumstances clouding their eyes.

All were seasoned veterans of the Battle of Roth and had willingly placed their lives in her hands when they chose to serve her. Wives and children anxiously awaited their safe return from this voyage while their leader stood impotent upon a crippled ship. Her hands clenched the railing as she faced the horizon, straining to see the portal doors and frantically calculating the time they had left to reach their journey's end.

Had it been her own foolishness dooming her ship and its crew? She could feel something was not right with that ship, yet she still let her pride in her ability to take care of her people push aside common sense. Did that somehow play a hand in their fate? But if that were the case, then why make her men suffer for their leader's wrongdoings? Why not let some sea serpent remove her from her command and deliver her crew safely to their loved ones? She could almost hear her father's solitary cry of disappointment at her shame when she realized the cry she heard was more real than dream.

Shaking her head to clear her thoughts, Ariana looked around to find the source of the sound. Low at first, then gaining in number and volume, the cries could soon be heard clearly as she rushed to the bow to gaze out over the moonlit water. Off the starboard side she could see the surface break as mermaids dove and leapt as they called out to each other. Her heart skipped a beat when she realized Prince Kaspar was in the lead and they were heading her way. What was he doing there? Had he come to mock her with the knowledge he was still free while she was held captive?

She should have known creatures of the sea would have the freedom to visit the Otherworld whenever they desired, while she was still bound by the moon's cycles and depended on its power to open the portal door. Oh, how he must hate her so to come watch her fate play out upon a place she had never wished to be.

Despite the anger beginning to churn in her stomach, she was still mesmerized by the beauty of the merman before her. Hair as dark as night seemed to shimmer in the moonlight as corded muscles pushed his body out of the water as he neared the side of the ship. The others had died down to silence and even her men quietly waited to see what their leader would do with this new turn of events. Leaning over the side, she looked down at Prince Kaspar and called out to him, "Why have you come here?"

"How are you doing this fine evening, Princess Ariana?"

How was she doing? He asked such a question like this was a chance meeting instead of a deliberate act of cruelty on his part? His words only served to feed her anger at his arrogance and there were heat in her words, "Leave this place! You are not welcome or needed here!"

Damn that smirk upon his lips as he smiled at her and replied, "Oh, fair lady, I would think I should be a most welcome sight at a time like this. I watched your heroic battle with that war ship but fear they may have gotten the best of you and your crew. Now you are faced with a new problem of how to return to Lunadar before the portal closes."

"How do you know about the portal anyway? I thought only my father knew of its existence."

"You think you are the only one to know of the moon's magic? Why, I've heard those legends ever since I could balance on my own tail, but what do mermaids need of such trickery? We are as free as the waves themselves to come and go as we please. We do not have to depend on a ship, even a crippled one, to get us back home."

Ariana could feel the heat flushing her cheeks as she listened to the prince's offhanded remark about her present predicament. Eyes flashing daggers at the merman, she retorted, "Since you can so easily make your way wherever you may desire, why not leave me in peace. This is no concern of yours!"

The smile slid from Prince Kaspar's lips as he replied, "Can you not set aside your pride for just a moment and think of your men? Must they pay for your moment of foolishness? I think perhaps I am just the creature you do need!"

It didn't matter she questioned her own pride mere moments before when she wondered if it was her curse to doom her men to a life apart from loved ones. How dare this merman accuse her of putting her own interest ahead of others! She was just about to demand Prince Kaspar leave her sight when she glanced at the men standing all around her. No longer did they hide the fear beginning to show in their eyes. They knew they were doomed to a life beyond Lunadar if this broken ship did not make it to the portal in time, but to the very last man, they would not raise a word against her.

She closed her eyes for a moment and tried to calm her anger at the truth in Prince Kaspar's words. How easily it would have been for her to send him away because she didn't want to lower herself to asking for his help. What a bitter pill to swallow pride can be. Ariana suspected he knew how hard it was for her to say these words and yet he did not mock her further when her shoulders drooped before turning back to him, "For my men and them alone I will accept your help, Prince Kaspar."

He merely nodded his head and turned to the mermaids gathered around him. A few words were spoken, and they raced from his side in all directions, stirring the waters with their departure. What could they do to save her ship? Time was ticking away and in the far distance she could see the moon dipping lower toward the horizon. Was this how it was to end? Would she never see her precious Candra again?

The faces of her men became blurred as she quickly blinked away the sting of tears. No time for self-pity now. She must stay strong for them and the memory of her father. And she must place her trust in someone who can't be trusted.

For once she couldn't protect her people and it was almost a physical pain to realize she would be forever indebted to Prince Kaspar. She had tried the past three years to erase his face from her memory, to forget him and his mermaid song, but the gods must like playing with her. Just when she thought herself done with him, there he stood before her at this year's Winter Solstice celebration. To tear open the wound once more with his silky voice before the queen threatened to make her pay because of some foolish mermaid law. And now he shadowed her once more.

This time as her rescuer even as every part of her yearned to scream out, "*Leave me be! Release me from your mermaid spell and return to the world from which you came!*" But instead, she stood upon her ship with her hands clenched by her side and glared at him while they both waited for what would happen next.

In the distance, softly at first, then growing stronger, she heard a sound she couldn't quite make out. Looking down at Price Kaspar's smiling face, it dawned on her from where their rescue would come. The water all around them began to dip and swirl as the giants of the sea raced in the ship's direction. Their song became louder as tail flukes cut through the water and slapped the surface as they surrounded the ship.

This was the miracle the merman had brought her. To be carried home on the backs of beasts like a princess in her carriage. Edging closer to the sides of the broken vessel, massive grey bodies nudged the ship until it balanced precariously upon their backs. Slowly at first and then picking up speed, the whales followed Prince Kaspar's command and headed for the distant horizon.

Once again Ariana could hear the mermaids calling out to each other as they raced in the ship's wake. She was powerless to do anything to help, and it did not sit well with her. The men begin to cheer in relief, and she could only glance back at Prince Kaspar before he faded into the distance as the whales made their way toward the portal and home. Ariana knew the moment between her and the merman was not over. There would come a time soon when she would still have to answer to him for this rescue he had brought her. She could feel it in her bones.

Could she be wrong about him? Her heart said no, but her logical mind was starting to doubt. How easily he could have left her to her fate. And how did he even come to be there in the first place? The ocean was vast between the two worlds and what were the chances he would be in the right place at the right time? Had he been following her? If so, to what purpose? Wouldn't it have solved the question of Candra's future for her mother to be lost at sea?

She first imagined he was looking for a sign of weakness to be used against her. But if that was the case, then why rescue her ship? She did not understand Prince Kaspar's motives but could only send a prayer of thanks to the gods she would not be held responsible for the loss of her men on this voyage. Now to make it safely home

and see to the repairs of her ship before she could hold
Candra in her arms again.

CHAPTER EIGHT

The light faded once more behind the portal as it closed behind them. Tails were raised in salute to Prince Kaspar as one by one, each whale blew a spray of water high into the air before sinking below the waves to return to their homes. She could feel her men breathe a sigh of relief as they made their way into their hidden cove. Repairs would have to wait as her men began to unload the precious cargo and she prepared to return home to Lunadar.

How foolish of her to think she could escape so easily. Just as she was about to bid her men farewell and wish them a safe journey to the castle after their work was completed, she heard a silky voice call out her name. Weary muscles tensed once more as she turned to face Prince Kaspar waiting at the ship's stern. Was she never to be released from this song quickening her breath and racing along her spine to awaken her senses to the creature before her? A smile tugged at the corner of his mouth to meet her frown as stormy eyes met cool green ones and she said, "What do you want of me, Prince Kaspar?"

"Well, for a start, a thank you would be welcomed."

"A 'thank you'?"

"Yes, milady. After all, I did save your life and the lives of your crew."

"Why you pompous, arrogant, self-deluded…"

She never got to finish her scathing retort as Prince Kaspar had the audacity to laugh at her. Princess Ariana! Leader of Lunadar! One of her hands balled into a fist as the other slid down her leg to rest near the dagger hidden in her boot. Prince Kaspar raised his open hands in defense as he fought hard to contain his merriment.

"Dear lady, I do apologize for laughing just now but I must confess, you look so righteous when there's fire in your eyes, and I simply couldn't resist."

The fool was mocking her, and she fought to regain control of her anger before she wasted any more energy on the prince. Ariana turned her back on him to leave. She thought she'd caught a glimpse of sadness shadow his own eyes as Prince Kaspar suddenly whispered "Why, Ariana? Why keep her existence from me?"

Like a dying wind, her anger evaporated and was replaced with a new, uncomfortable feeling. Shame. Shame at having once thought she might trust this creature before her. Shame at the circumstances forcing her to be deceitful. This merman before her may be fickle by nature but he was in truth Candra's father and had the right to know of her existence.

Ariana could feel the moisture gathering in her eyes and kept her face turned away from him before replying,

"I had no choice. Queen Naab would have done exactly as she threatened to do at the ball. She would make me pay for being ensnared by your mermaid song by trying to take my daughter from me."

"But she is my child, too! She has the right to know of the royal mermaid blood flowing through her veins. What is her name, Ariana? I have the right to know at least that much!"

Ariana turned her head to look at Prince Kaspar through misty eyes and contemplated telling him her daughter's name. What would it hurt? It was already too late to erase a chance meeting so what if he knew what she called her?

"I named her Candra."

Prince Kaspar closed his eyes for a moment and it looked as if he was conjuring up the memory of that first meeting with his child to see if the name fit her before finally opening his eyes to stare deep into her own.

"Thank you for telling me. Despite what you think of me, I have fathered no other children, and Candra is as much an heir to the mermaid world as the mystic, even though her own mother might wish it otherwise."

She tilted her head and studied him closely as she thought about what he just said. In her haste to secure Candra's safety, she never stopped to realize his words might be true. Candra didn't just have Ariana's own mystical powers to rely on but might also have the powers of the deep. It made Ariana wonder for a moment what she might be able to do in time to serve and protect the people of Lunadar? But become leader of the mermaid kingdom? Never!

"What you say may be true, Prince Kaspar, but it was not a legacy of her own choosing nor mine. You took away my right to choose at that Winter Solstice ball when you placed me under your mermaid spell. Your own mother plots to take her from her home to live with the creatures of your world.

Even now you gloat at the prospect that I am indebted to you for helping us to get home and this 'thank you' you seek is but one way to remind me of my place in your world under your thumb instead of by your side as an equal. But as the leader of Lunadar, I promise you and your queen will never be allowed anywhere near my daughter!"

Storm clouds began to brew in his eyes as Prince Kaspar rose on his tail to his full height until he was almost nose to nose with Ariana before replying, "You misjudge me harshly, milady, and one day you will realize it but by then it may be too late. Yes, Candra is of my blood and yes, I believe she should know well the realm of her father's kingdom, but not at the price of her mother's love!

As far as saving your men, we both know your ship was doomed and unable to make it to the portal in time without my help. Is your pride so important to you that you would risk not only your life, but the lives of your men, just to prove you have no need of me? And you of all people should know that once you have heard the mermaid's song, you can but only allow the song to play out before the spell might be broken."

Prince Kaspar ran a hand through his hair before continuing, "Why do you think I returned to the ball when I did? Running from our fates does not free us from them, Ariana. There is always a price to pay for the foolishness of one's youth, so why not face the song head on and see what the future may bring?"

There it was again. Her heart warred with her mind as she listened to his words, and all that was left was doubt as to whether she could truly trust him. The song he spoke of was clearly heard in the wind and morning mist surrounding them. All she had to do was surrender to it and Prince Kaspar would protect his daughter's future with his life. The only price to be paid would be her spirit's freedom to choose her own fate.

She'd never know what she might have replied because all at once the tension between them was broken by Alasdair shouting her name as he raced on horseback over the cobblestone to the water's edge, leading Aramid behind him. Turning her back on the prince, Ariana quickly went to her captain, already fighting the fear snaking its way through her belly to rest in her heart.

"Princess Ariana, you must return to Lunadar at once. Your daughter has vanished!"

Ariana rushed from the shoreline to quickly mount her stallion.

"When did this happen? Who has taken her?"

Alasdair quickly glanced towards the ship before looking back at her. She could sense his hesitation and there was a sharpness in her tone as she said, "Alasdair, I command you to tell me at once what has happened to my daughter!"

The captain of her troops lowered his eyes before replying, "Queen Naab has captured her, milady."

Her head whipped in the direction of the merman, just in time to catch what might have been a look of surprise cross his features, but in her fear and anger she did not care. Reaching for her dagger, she pointed it at Prince Kaspar's heart and said, "To think I ever considered trusting you! A black-hearted creature of the deep is what you are and what you will always be! I swear on my father's grave if one hair on Candra's head has been harmed by your people, I will take your mother's life first and then return for your own!"

Ariana didn't even wait for his reply as she dug her heels into Aramid's side and raced towards the castle with Alasdair in her wake. All she could think was how did this happen? Was Lord Shemar's hatred for her and her people not enough? Must she lose her daughter as well?

She feared she treated her faithful steed badly in her haste to reach the castle, but the bile rose in her throat as she returned to Lunadar. Throwing the reins to her stable hand with a command to see to her horse, she leapt from Aramid's back and took the steps two at a time in the direction of the nursery. as she shouted for her manservant.

She saw some of the villagers gathered in the great hall. Their looks of astonishment at her attire would have been humorous if it weren't for the fear threatening to overwhelm her. Leaving her people to wonder over her manly attire, Ariana quickly made her way to Candra's chambers where Macklebee stood by the doorway. It took all she had to push down the fear threatening to choke her and concentrate on Macklebee as she stepped into her daughter's bedroom. Bowing low and wringing his hands, the servant's voice trembled as the words tumbled from his mouth.

"Princess Ariana, it is my fault your daughter is gone. I only took my eyes off her but for a moment to speak to the cook about the morning meal. When I turned around Candra had disappeared! She somehow got outside and even though the guards knew not to let her go beyond the castle walls, no one thought Queen Naab might send sprites to our waterfalls to spirit your daughter away. Alasdair and the troops have searched everywhere but we fear Queen Naab has taken her back to her castle at Renndar!"

Ariana barely heard Macklebee's words over the roaring in her ears. How could Prince Kaspar deceive her like this? Why bother saving her ship while Queen Naab stole her daughter from her? Why not simply let the portal close and doom them forever on the seas of the Otherworld? She did not understand the game he played yet she swore she would return Candra to safety.

Only another mother would understand the warring emotions threatening to overwhelm Ariana. Fear she would never touch skin as soft as rose petals again when gathering Candra in her arms. Blinding anger over Queen Naab's deception. But mostly frustration over how she would deal with Prince Kaspar. If she had her way, he would wish he never played his mermaid song for her!

If she were a man, her fury could be unleashed, and her people would think it nothing more than the right of their leader. But in their eyes, she would always be a woman first before their leader. There were times she wished the deck of her ship were beneath her feet once again.

On the ocean her men did not question her actions, nor did they expect her to quake at the thought of battle. A false calm cloaked her spirit as she looked at her faithful servant. While it may be his fault for letting Candra leave the castle, how could she blame him for what she herself could not control?

Candra had the inquisitiveness of a newborn foal and could be slippery as an eel to keep track of. It was always a challenge to keep her strong-willed child within

Lunadar's walls. But this was something she had feared most since she knew she would have a child destined to hear the song of the deep calling out to her. Ariana just never expected her daughter to be taken from her so soon and not by the hands of the queen. She had to ask Macklebee another question before she gathered her troops to go in search of her daughter.

"How do you know it was Queen Naab who took my child?"

Reaching deep inside his vest, Macklebee slowly withdrew a large strand of seaweed and handed it to her with trembling fingers. Taking it from him, she looked down at the strange handwriting and began to read:

Daughter of King Midar,

Your father turned his back on my council years ago when he forged his alliance with Queen Elysie. He wouldn't heed my words when I warned him such a union would only lead to his downfall. Now you, his daughter and a mere mystic, think yourself wiser than myself? Who are you to think you could hide forever the result of a forbidden union such as this?

You know nothing of the gifts that child might possess and even if only half mermaid, she will take her rightful place as heir to Renndar's throne! Even now, we prepare to initiate Mordona, as she will forever be called, in two days' time for the water test of our people to see if she has true mermaid blood flowing through her veins.

Queen Naab

She released the seaweed to let it flutter to the floor as she turned to look at Macklebee, "What was this alliance Queen Naab speaks of between Queen Elysie and my father?"

"I know not, milady."

"Are you sure?"

"Yes, Princess Ariana. This is the first I have heard of such a thing."

She strode to the doorway and called for Alasdair who had been waiting in the great hall with the villagers. She asked him the same question, but he was as confused as her manservant about this supposed union between her father and the queen of Quallan Forest. Why would they need to form such a union? Did it have anything to do with the debt Queen Elysie said was finally repaid when she led her to the portal linking their two kingdoms? All she knew was she had less than two days to find the answers and save her daughter.

"Alasdair gather the men and be ready to ride in twenty minutes time."

"Of course, milady, but where do we ride?"

"To get answers from Queen Elysie!"

CHAPTER NINE

Ariana had not used the land portal since she last spoke to the Fairie queen, but Aramid still remembered the way. She was sure her men thought her mad. If not for the fear of Candra's safety gnawing at her insides she would have thought herself mad as well. She knew of the possible consequences once she entered Quallan Forest unannounced again, but she knew Queen Elysie was the only one who could give her the answers to her questions. It was a risk she was willing to take.

Stopping just short of the entrance of the portal, she raised her hand to halt her men. Alasdair continued to her side before saying, "Surely, milady, you do not plan to make this journey on your own?"

"Yes, I do. It has occurred to me I was foolish to think I can just walk up to Queen Elysie with a troop of guards and demand an audience. I will not endanger my men to justify what might be my greatest folly. My daughter's life is in danger and there are secrets in Quallan Forest which might help return her to me. Now do as I command!"

Shoulders slumped in resignation as Alastair bowed his head and turned his mount back toward the waiting men. Squaring her shoulders, Ariana nudged Aramid forward. Candra was but a child, with a child's fears, and Ariana could only imagine she must think her mother abandoned her. And what would happen if Queen Naab performed the water test? It would be no huge loss to the queen should Candra not survive. Just another casualty of the times they must endure. But for Ariana? It would be like losing the very air she breathed.

Vegetation seemed to close around her as she stepped through the portal and emerged deep within Quallan Forest. The creatures of this kingdom sensed her presence even if they could not see her and once again they would wonder why the stranger from Lunadar had returned. She hesitated on the stairs, trying to decide whether to stay where she was or go in search of the Fairie queen.

Surely, she must know by now Ariana had entered her world once more. Would she be as merciful as the last time they met? She didn't have long to wonder as the sudden, deafening stillness announced the queen's arrival. Ariana glanced to her right and noticed the trees gave way as Queen Elysie glided across the forest floor to stop before Ariana.

The Fairie queen must not fear many outsiders entering her realm as her guards remained well hidden behind the trees surrounding them. Ariana dropped to her knees and placed her forehead on her outstretched arms but not before she saw the fury coiling in Queen

Elysie's eyes, ready to strike at the slightest move Ariana might make.

"Foolish girl! I warned you my debt to your father's memory had been repaid when I showed you this portal and I owe you nothing else. What is the meaning of this intrusion?"

Her voice was barely above a serpent's hiss, yet it echoed throughout the forest and all creatures trembled, including Ariana.

"I beg you, Queen Elysie, please forgive me. I have nowhere else to turn and seek your council."

"Your battles with Lord Shemar do not concern me or my people. I see no reason to help you, despite the fact we share the same enemy. That alone is not reason enough to put my own kingdom at risk to come to your aid. Now go!"

She knew in an instant if she did nothing, her daughter's fate would be sealed. Risking her own life as well as the future of Lunadar, she did what no one had ever done before in the history of their times. Rising to her feet, Ariana stood before the Fairie queen and looked into two pools of dark green fire. Taking the queen's silence as a good omen, Ariana stood even taller and quietly spoke from her heart.

"Queen Elysie, I beseech you. I would never have come here were it not my last hope. I have tried in all these years since my father's death to be an honest and dutiful leader of my people while asking nothing in return but to share in their happiness.

Lord Shemar has done everything in his power to destroy Lunadar and yet we still manage to survive. But now Queen Naab also seeks to destroy Lunadar as well by taking the one thing I place higher than my duty to my people, even higher than my duty to my father's memory."

The void after Ariana's passionate speech was almost deafening to her own ears as she struggled to halt the sudden tears beginning to slide down her cheeks. She didn't know if her words had any effect on the Fairie queen, yet she sensed Queen Elysie was judging the truth behind Ariana's plea. Once again, she heard the soft hiss of the queen's voice as her words echoed through the forest.

"What is this thing you place higher than the memory of a great king?"

"My daughter."

Was it her imagination or did she hear the soft intake of breath by Queen Elysie? *Was that a hint of fear suddenly radiating in the air around them? But what would one as powerful as the Fairie queen have to fear?* Ariana watched the queen's eyes turn from green fire to dark black as the forest around her began to glow even brighter. What had she done to cause such an instant change?

"Come!"

Ariana soon found herself rushing through Quallan Forest as she raced to keep up with Queen Elysie. She didn't know where they were headed, but even the creatures of the kingdom were retreating deeper into the shadows to get out of their path. They entered a part of the forest Ariana had not been before. Ahead of them, rising from the forest floor, was a structure shimmering in sunlight filtering through the treetops. Emerald encrusted stone walls with high towers in each corner made her realize she was about to enter the fairie queen's castle.

While growing up, Ariana had always heard whispers about Quallan Castle. It was the center of the queen's power and an impressive fortress. Her own father used to tell her stories about this magical place. Fairie Tales, he used to call them, but now she was beginning to wonder just how much he knew about this forest kingdom and the creatures who lived there.

Upon entering the castle, she expected Queen Elysie to take her to a throne room but instead they traveled down corridor after corridor until she feared she would never be able to find her way out again. That was, if she would even be allowed to ever leave that place. Of all the tales told about Quallan Castle, she had never actually heard any accounts of exactly what might go on inside those walls.

Fairies were rumored to be timid creatures, so Ariana was not surprised to encounter no one along the way, but she could still sense their presence all around her. What did they know that she did not? Finally, they turned a corner and came to a heavily guarded door at the end of a long hallway. One look from the queen and guards melted into the shadows as if they had never been standing there.

Nothing could prepare Ariana for what she saw when Queen Elysie passed through the door and she followed. Large sconces decorated every wall as hundreds of lit candles bathed everything in an almost unnatural glow. Large trees decorated each side of the only window and the faint scent of jasmine hung in the air though she saw no blossoms.

In the very center of the room stood what appeared to be some type of shrine but to whom or what she knew not. The Fairie queen silently looked at the few items lying on the table and whispered some words Ariana could not understand. Then turning to her for the first time since they left the portal, Queen Elysie's voice had regained the soft, musical quality Ariana remembered from past Winter Solstice celebrations as the queen began to speak.

"Who fathered the child?"

Her question momentarily surprised Ariana and she could only look into eyes no longer blackened by anger but reflecting the candle's light like deep emeralds as Queen Elysie waited for an answer. Ariana wondered how much she could safely reveal about Candra's heritage. Ariana did not trust the Fairie queen but gave the only answer she could.

"Prince Kaspar."

Did she imagine the slight sagging of the queen's shoulders as she heard a whisper of a sigh? Why should she care about who fathered her daughter, and would Ariana ever discover who was honored by this shrine?

"It is as I thought."

"What do you mean?

Instead of answering her question, Queen Elysie waved a hand toward the table and asked one of her own.

"Do you not recognize anything here?"

Ariana looked closer at the table and began to realize those were some of her father's things lying there. She did not understand what she saw before her and she didn't even try to halt her questions as she turned to face the queen.

"Why do you honor my father so? What has he done to deserve this? Why is it so important to know my daughter's lineage?"

A raised hand silenced her outburst and there appeared to be a ghost of a smile on the queen's lips. Ariana's eyes widened as the queen's melodious voice began to spin a tale more fantastic than any she had heard at her father's knee.

"King Midar was a great champion of Quallan Forest and the creatures who live here. You were right in thinking the king and I had formed an alliance with the common goal of protecting that which was most precious to both of us."

"Our kingdoms?"

"The heirs to our thrones."

Ariana must not have heard correctly. "You have an heir?"

"Yes. A daughter. You have met her before though you did not realize it at the time. Her identity is Princess Tomari."

For a moment she was completely stunned by this revelation. The high priestess was rightful heir to the throne of Quallan Forest? This was but one of many secrets her father seemed to have kept from her. What others might be revealed?

"On the eve of your birth, your father came to me with a wish to form an alliance between our two kingdoms. I knew King Midar to be an honorable and respected leader of his people, so I entrusted my greatest secret with him when we sealed our pact."

"Why was I never told of this?"

"Your father knew the danger my daughter would be in should anyone discover her identity."

"What kind of danger?"

"Tomari's father was the mermaid king."

She was shocked by this information. As one who had felt Queen Naab's fury, she suddenly felt sorry for the Fairie queen. Ariana's heart bled for her as she knew what it felt like to love a child yet not be able to claim her to the world as her own. But what did this have to do with her father? There was one question she must ask.

"Does Queen Naab know?"

"No. If she did, she would stop at nothing to lay claim to Tomari and that is something I will never allow!"

"What part did my own father play in this?"

"Have you never wondered the reason for my hatred of Lord Shemar? Two moons before the Battle of Roth, the dark lord kidnapped Tomari while she was at Dreydan's Falls. He thought her merely my high priestess, and a prize worthy of Queen Naab's alliance should he deliver such a gem to her. Lord Shemar played his hand well as my guards are no match for his Drundles on dry land and he would never have attempted to enter my forest on his own.

Queen Naab has always hungered to rule beyond the ocean realm, so what better way than to control the land kingdoms as well? But as powerful as I am within my own kingdom, I knew my daughter would become a pawn in Queen Naab's ruthless fight for absolute power should Lord Shemar be successful in delivering Tomari to her."

"So, my father became the champion in your stead?"

"King Midar volunteered to rescue my daughter from Lord Shemar. He alone might have been strong enough to fight the Drundles and return Tomari to me. The gods favored your father that day and Lord Shemar was furious. He swore revenge for your father's brave deed.

Having lost his leverage against me, the dark lord then conspired to steal even something more sacred to Quallan Forest than my daughter and once again your father came to my rescue. This infuriated Lord Shemar and two months later, King Midar paid with his own life for his act of bravery in the face of such odds."

Ariana could not help the tears from clouding her eyes. "Now my own child is in danger and who will be my champion?"

"Queen Naab knows of your daughter's existence?"

"Candra is a prisoner of the queen even as we speak. She will force my daughter to endure the mermaid's water test, and I fear the outcome. My daughter honors the mystic part of her heritage, yet I know not how strong the call of the mermaid may be within her. Queen Naab swears to perform the test in two days' time and will do everything in her power to keep my child from me! It is why I had come to seek your wise council and would even beg for your help if need be."

The Fairie queen turned to look at the shrine once more and seemed lost in thought. Would she place her own people in harm's way for the sake of a child she had never seen? Was the affection she felt for her father's memory strong enough to extend help to his daughter?

Ariana felt as if the entire forest kingdom held its breath as they all awaited Queen Elysie's reply. Time was flying past and she was sure Alasdair wondered what had become of her, but he would never disobey her command to wait for her return. Just as she was about to give up all hope, the Fairie queen turned to her and she could see the determination in her eyes.

"I, queen of Quallan Forest and trusted ally of King Midar, will help you rescue your daughter from Queen Naab. We must quickly make plans before another hour passes!"

Ariana did not realize she had been holding her breath as she waited for Queen Elysie's answer to her plea. She clasped her suddenly trembling hands to still them and tried to steady the butterflies in her stomach. To have the Fairie queen as her ally was a gift far greater than any she could have hoped for. Quickly they discussed how they would rescue Candra from Queen Naab and soon Ariana was riding Aramid back to her men as they stood anxiously awaiting her safe return.

Though he gave away nothing, Ariana could sense her captain's relief as he bowed his head when she drew up to his side.

"You have returned safely, milady."

"Indeed, I have Alasdair and I bring with me great news. Queen Elysie has pledged her help in rescuing my daughter. Let us return to Lunadar immediately as we have much planning to do. Queen Naab will soon be regretting her decision to take what belongs to me!"

CHAPTER TEN

In just two short hours they had gathered the weapons they needed to do battle. Queen Elysie's magic was strong, but even her power would not last forever. The elixir she had prepared for them to drink would give them the ability to breathe underwater for only twenty-four hours. Only one day's time to uncover her daughter's hiding place and return her to the safety of Lunadar. Ariana had to believe the gods would not let them get this far to dash their hopes like waves against the cliffs.

Queen Elysie and her warriors were waiting at the water's edge for them. The same determination could be found in their eyes as in Ariana's and her men's. The fairie warriors lived to serve their queen in the same way as Ariana's men served her, and they all served the future of their respective kingdoms. Candra was her life and Lunadar's future. Nothing would stop her from holding her daughter safely in her arms once more.

Gulping down the murky green, foul-tasting potion, they slowly descended seven leagues beneath the waves. Queen Naab's castle lay on the edge of Renndar and surprise would be on their side.

Never had a land walker presumed to enter Queen Naab's world, so she would have a false sense of security. The water tests she planned to perform involved a series of challenges mermaid children must go through as proof of their right to remain in Renndar and under Queen Naab's protection. But what of the offspring of Prince Kaspar and potential heir to the mermaid throne? That child would be subject not only to the water test but also a test to determine their future right to lead the mermaids. Ariana had heard rumors of such a test possibly ending in death. Especially when someone of less than pure mermaid blood was forced to participate. What chance did Candra have? Her blood was only half mermaid, and only the gods knew for certain whether it was in her destiny to rule Renndar.

Slowly they began to make out the seaweed covered walls of Queen Naab's castle. Only a small band of trident-carrying soldiers guarded the outside, and the invaders made short work of them before any alarm could be raised. It was not their wish to take the lives of the people of Renndar, but what sacrifices would be made was up to the queen's resistance to their rescue attempt. Leaving a few of the men to guard the mermaid soldiers, they silently entered the castle.

Without speaking, Queen Elysie motioned for Ariana to search the northern and western hallways while she and her men searched the other ones. All preparations would likely to be going on in the courtyards just beyond the throne room which left them with easier access to the rest of the castle. They would probably keep Candra locked away in some outer chamber, preparing her for the moment the tests confirmed her royal mermaid blood, and Ariana's only chance to rescue her would be before the ceremony took place.

All the rooms were empty as they quietly made their way down the corridor. Ariana's heartbeat quickened, and her stomach clinched as she realized there was only one door left to open. She didn't know if Queen Elysie had found her daughter or if Candra lay behind the door before her.

Raising her hand to halt her men, she slowly tested the handle and took a calming breath as it smoothly turned under her clenched fingers. Cautiously pushing it open, she peered inside and discovered her daughter quietly sitting on a small stool in front of a shell shaped dresser. Mermaids were combing and braiding her long black hair while weaving seashells among the streak of white so much like her own.

She wanted to rush into the room but years of pirating on the high seas made her cautious. *Why did Candra not fight to free herself from her captors?* Noticing her half-closed eye lids for the first time, Ariana realized Queen Naab wouldn't take chances the possible heir to her throne escaping before the tests proving her rightful place as future leader of Renndar were completed. Candra had been given a calming potion to help keep her subdued. How dare Queen Naab do that to her child!

No longer caring, Ariana burst into the room, causing the mermaids to scream in surprise and terror at the look on her face. She knew she had mere minutes before more of the queen's soldiers would come to their rescue. She had to get Candra to safety.

Pushing the mermaids aside, Ariana gathered her child in her arms as she shouted to her men before racing back down the corridors toward the castle entrance. Cursing at the twists and turns of every hallway, Ariana worried if they would make it in time.

Suddenly she saw flashing lights lighting up the corridor, calling the mermaids to battle. The only means of escape was quickly blocked by Queen Naab's men and the sound of battle rang out in the hallway as soldiers fought against Ariana's men.

Shoving Candra into a corner behind her, Ariana drew her sword just in time to parry as an enemy's blade was hell bent on sending her to a watery grave. All around the room grunts of the fight and cries from the wounded could be heard. Metal clashed against metal as each side made a desperate attempt to overpower the other.

Pulling her dagger from her boot, Ariana quickly thrust it into the side of the merman in front of her and shoved him to the side with one arm as she grabbed Candra with the other. She was beginning to wonder if

Queen Elysie had abandoned her when she saw the fairie queen's men rush in from the other hallway.

Trapped between the two armies, there was initial confusion on the mermaids' faces as Ariana realized they hadn't expected more than one enemy in their midst. One by one the mermen fell beneath swords as Ariana and Queen Elysie slowly inched their way toward the door leading outside. Soon the rough surface of their exit was against her back and Ariana shouted to her men to not give up. The gods seemed to be favoring them that day and victory would soon be theirs.

Turning to make sure Candra was still safely out of harm's way, Ariana barely heard the slicing sound the trident made as it flew from Queen Naab's bow and straight toward her own heart. Only turning to check on her daughter's safety prevented the barb from finding its deadly mark. Instead, she felt raw burning pain exploding through her left shoulder as the shaft buried deep into her flesh. Ariana pulled at the door with adrenaline filled muscles and shoved Candra outside before following her to stumble into the waiting arms of Prince Kaspar.

Ariana should have known he would be lurking in the corners, too much a coward to defend his own home from intruders. She struggled to release his embrace but was losing blood quickly. The world around her began to tilt and swirl.

It took all her will to remain standing, even with the prince's help. Ariana barely noticed the others following them as Prince Kaspar pulled Candra by her arm while half carrying, half dragging Ariana away from the castle and to safety.

As if from afar, she heard the soft hiss of Queen Elysie's voice mingle with Prince Kaspar's as their two voices clashed in debate. She couldn't tell if they were talking about her and yet she got the sense the queen was somehow testing him, questioning his motives as Ariana had since the very first time she met him.

Desperately she looked around for Candra, using her good arm to struggle to get free of the arms now fighting to keep her still. Ariana looked up into two green eyes darkened with worry or anger, she didn't know which. Opening her mouth to insist he release her, Ariana was surprised at how weak her voice had become.

"Where is my child? I demand you let go of me."

A ghost of a smile touched one corner of his mouth before Prince Kaspar quickly replied,

"While I would love to stand around and exchange pleasantries with you, milady, we have more pressing matters to attend to. Our daughter is safe, and you are losing too much blood to stand on your own. Besides we must leave this place before my mother realizes who has come to your aid!"

She wanted to tell the prince she had no need of his assistance, but his voice was coming from a faraway place, and a dark curtain began to slide over her. Ariana felt herself lifted into strong arms and was surprised by the immediate feeling of warmth coursing through her body, tempting her to let go and fall into the abyss. She had no choice but to obey the temptation.

CHAPTER ELEVEN

Had Ariana merely dreamed of the battle at Renndar? She could not tell if hours or days had passed since they fought Queen Naab's soldiers. She thought she could hear her daughter's voice coming towards her as if from a great distance, but when she tried to reach for her, her arms were made of stone, and she could only moan as the pain in her shoulder ripped through her body.

She struggled weakly against the hands holding her down and cried out as they removed the trident. Now all that could be done was to wait and pray to the gods for mercy. Many a brave warrior had died at the end of a triton's weapon, and only time would tell if Ariana would be spared. In a fever-filled haze, Ariana saw a monster rise above turbulent waters. A sea creature with deep green eyes coming to steal her heart and take the thing she cherished most. She struggled against the arms holding her tightly against a too warm body as her fever spiked. Finally, she tumbled into a deep sleep as the sound of the mermaid's song whispered to her.

Days later bright sunlight poured into her bed chambers to warm her face, Ariana opened her eyes to see Macklebee hovering over her, fear clouding his eyes.

When he saw she was awake, a smile split his face in two, and he quickly wiped the sudden moisture from his eyes.

"Oh, Princess Ariana, I have been overcome with fear at the thought of you dying from that trident."

She tried to roll over onto her side, but the pain in her shoulder quickly told her at least some of her dreams had been real. She eased back against the pillows and cautiously tried her voice,

"Macklebee, how long have I been in bed?"

"Almost a week, milady."

"A week? How can that be? Where is Candra? Is she safe?"

Macklebee shushed and clucked at her like a mother hen.

"There, there, milady, everything is well. The little one is safe in her chambers. You have been fighting the fevers ever since Prince Kaspar and Queen Elysie returned you to Lunadar."

"Prince Kaspar? Here?" Now she remembered. The battle. Her wound. Falling into his arms. She tried in vain to suppress the flush she felt staining her cheeks and quickly changed the subject.

"Bring me my daughter, Macklebee."

"But milady, what you need now is rest."

"Macklebee! Am I not in charge here? I demand you bring Candra to me this instant!"

She instantly regretted her harsh words as Macklebee scurried from the bedchamber to return with her daughter. The simple act of raising her voice had left her feeling lightheaded. She was glad for the sudden silence while she tried to regain her equilibrium before her manservant returned.

Gingerly, she eased into a sitting position and marveled at the fact that so much time had passed her by. What of her people? And what of Lord Shemar and the Drundles? Surely, he could have attempted another attack on the people of Lunadar if he knew its leader was wounded?

Her mind skirted around the one person she didn't want to think about, but she knew she could not hide from him forever. What of Prince Kaspar? Why had he rescued her? And why did he return his daughter to Lunadar when Ariana's death and her capture could only have given Queen Naab the revenge she sought? She feared she would never have the answers to her questions. She also feared she would never be free of the cursed mermaid's song connecting their two spirits.

The sound of childish laughter broke into Ariana's thoughts, and she saw her child's eyes lit up as she raced into the room to crawl onto her mother's bed. Oh, the sweet joy of holding her child close to her! The pain in her shoulder was nothing compared to the pain she would feel if she'd lost her daughter.

Tucking Candra in close to her uninjured shoulder, she glanced at Macklebee hovering by the door and motioned him to return to her bedside. Ariana needed to ease this tension between them as it was not his fault. She lashed out at him because of her own need to see her daughter.

"Macklebee, I'm sorry for my harsh words of before."

"It is nothing, milady."

"No, I allowed my fear for my daughter's safety to overrule my better judgment. I know you have my best interests at heart, but you must realize with a week of my life lost to me, I must know of any news of late."

"Yes, milady."

"Please summon Alasdair to the great hall and have my lady's maid bring me something to wear."

"But milady."

"I know, I know. I feel weak as a kitten, but it will do my people good to see their leader back on her feet as quickly as possible, don't you think?"

"As you wish, milady."

She watched as her manservant left the room before turning to her daughter. Looking into her eyes, Ariana couldn't help but wonder at her daughter's resilience. A mere week ago she was being held captive in Queen

Naab's castle, facing possible death for the sake of a throne, and now she sought to play a tickle game with her mother as if it were normal for an almost three-year-old to suffer such things.

They played for a while before her sense of duty forced her away from her child. Her legs were wobbly like a newborn foal's as she slowly made her way to her window overlooking those lifesaving waterfalls. Candra had returned to her nursery and for a moment Ariana was alone with her thoughts tumbling around in a jumbled mess.

So much had happened in such a short time she barely had time to catch her breath. Was this how her life would always be? Struggling to keep her people safe? Forever looking over her shoulder and wondering when Lord Shemar or his Drundles will rise like evil spirits to haunt any chance of happiness she might have?

She closed her eyes to the beauty of the waterfalls and leaned wearily against the window's edge. Soon she would be trapped in those dreaded gowns with corsets stealing what little breath she had left. She didn't even have the energy to walk to where her lady's maid had prepared her bath. Suddenly she noticed the air around her felt different; almost as if supercharged with energy. What began as a mere whisper on the wind was now calling to her with full throated song. Would she never be rid of that watery devil?

Looking into the waters surrounding the castle, she found inquisitive eyes staring back at her and watching her every move.

"Princess Ariana, it does my heart good to see you up and about this fine day. I hope you have recovered well from your injury?"

As always, whenever she was near him she felt her pulse begin to race. Ignoring the impulse to retreat and the wincing pain shooting through her bandaged shoulder, her back was ramrod straight as she stared back at the merman before her.

"What do you want, Prince Kaspar? And why have you remained at Lunadar?" She could now see a hint of mischief twinkling in those eyes as he tried to suppress a grin.

"Why, is that any way to treat a guest at your home, milady? Surely, someone who had been saved from death not once but twice could offer just a wee bit more hospitality to their hero? A simple thank you would do nicely."

"You…you pompous oaf! What need have I to thank you? I was perfectly capable of taking care of myself at Renndar without your help!"

"Oh really? And to think I risked banishment from Renndar just to save your pretty little neck after you were almost killed by my mother's guards. And all you dare do now is stand there like some arrogant royal looking down on pond scum? Far better to look first in the mirror, milady, before you begin judging the worthiness of others!"

Ariana could almost feel the scorching heat from Prince Kaspar's words as she watched the churning waters announce his departure. Suddenly exhaustion flooded her body, and she sank against the window's edge.

She was so tired of seeing that taunting devil every time she turned around. So tired of fighting the urge to answer the mermaid's song. After what just happened at Renndar, Prince Kaspar should have been the sworn enemy of Lunadar. Yet each time she was around him she found it increasingly difficult to ignore her treacherous heart's desire. Only distance between them would help cool her blood and stay her course of securing the future of Lunadar.

Her lady's maid helped her to her bath, and she slowly lowered herself into the lavender scented waters. She wished nothing more than to escape this heavy yoke of responsibility her father's murder put on her shoulders, but she could not. Somewhere beyond Lunadar's waterfalls Lord Shemar and his Drundles were planning yet another attack upon Lunadar.

She could feel it in her bones as surely as she could feel her own mystic powers. She was a bit surprised the dark lord hadn't struck before now, and with all that had happened recently she was ashamed to realize the thought of avenging her father's death had been pushed to the back of her mind.

Suddenly eager to know the latest of Lord Shemar's whereabouts, she rushed through her bath as quickly as she could and endured the ritual of corset and laces as she was strapped into yet another dress to be paraded in front of her subjects like some peacock. Only a few more days existed before they slipped through the portal once again, and she would don more pleasing garments for the task at hand of feeding her people.

Later, as she made her way down the stairs to the great hall, she saw Alasdair striding across the room in her direction. The purposeful gait and frown on his face told her this was not good news he was bringing. Every muscle in her body quickly clenched and she winced as the stitches in her shoulder protested the sudden movement.

"What is it, Alasdair?"

The captain of her guards bowed low in response before replying, "How are you feeling, milady? Are you rested?"

Ariana couldn't hold back the sharpness of her tongue as she fought a sudden surge of lightheadedness from the tight corset at her waist.

"Do not toy with me! What news do you have?"

Alasdair snapped to attention at the steel in Ariana's voice and quickly shared the report his second in command had just relayed to him.

"It's Lord Shemar, milady. He and his Drundles have attacked one of the villages outside the protection of Lunadar's walls."

Ariana let her hand rest on the table next to her to steady herself before asking the question she dreaded the most whenever the dark lord was discussed.

"Any life lost?"

Alasdair looked to the floor before replying, "Aye. Most of the homes were destroyed and those who didn't meet their end by way of the Drundles' barbs were cut down like dogs by Lord Shemar himself!"

For a moment Ariana thought she would be ill, but she forced the taste of bile back down as she looked beyond the man standing in front of her to the people of Lunadar waiting in the room just beyond. Waiting for their leader to appear. But what kind of leader could she call herself?

A village was destroyed. Lives lost. And a taunt given from the dark lord himself as if he had the power to take life whenever he chose while standing in the shadow of the great waterfall city. Would this madness ever cease?

Every part of her wanted to turn her back on this new tragedy. To crawl back into her chambers as if to lick her wounds and never come out again. But her father had taught her to be strong, to stand firm in the face of danger and to never show your enemy any sign of weakness. Someday the tide would turn in her favor and Lord

Shemar would be made to pay for his crimes against Lunadar, of that she was certain. But for now, Ariana must continue to show her people they have a right to have faith in her ability to lead them out of this present darkness.

Turning toward Alasdair, Ariana straightened her shoulders back even more and with words tinged with pain, told her captain, "Have Aramid saddled at once and brought to the kitchens for me."

"But, milady, your injury has not had time to heal properly!" Alasdair replied in protest.

"I'm aware of my wound, Alasdair, as well as my duty to the people who depend upon their leader to be strong even at a time such as this. Now, do as I command and bring me my stallion!"

"As you wish, milady."

As Alasdair exited the hallway to do her bidding, Ariana took a moment to lean against the edge of the table and catch her breath. That corset was going to be the death of her; she was sure of it. Preparing Aramid would give her just enough time to change clothes and slip out back, unnoticed by the others. While the villagers may grumble about having to wait to see their leader, they would not be so forgiving should they see that same leader in riding breeches and a man's waistcoat.

CHAPTER TWELVE

The smell of death almost overwhelmed Ariana the closer she rode toward the charred remains of the village. On any other day Aramid would have been a handful, but the weakness in her shoulder coupled with the lightheadedness threatening to return with each prancing step the stallion took made Ariana grip the reins tighter, slowing the animal to a stop.

Just a scattering of thatch huts made up the village commons, but Lord Shemar made quick work to destroy everything in his path. Men lay near farm tools they used in a poor attempt to defend the women and children from those poisonous barbs. Mothers huddled over infants. Blinking eyes suddenly moist with tears, Ariana turned to Alasdair.

"When did this happen?"

Alasdair surveyed the carnage once more before replying, "Just before daybreak this morning, milady."

"But why wasn't I informed of this immediately? I could have done something to prevent this!"

"Milady, there was nothing you could have done to save them from their fate. What good would it have served for you to rise from your injuries to fight for these poor souls? It was already too late when the guards first told me what happened. How would your own sure death have changed the outcome of today's tragedy?"

Ariana momentarily rested her forehead on Aramid's withers. Alasdair was right. Hand to hand combat with the Drundles without water nearby was sheer suicide. Those poor villagers never had a chance once Lord Shemar decided their lives held no value. But that didn't mean her own helpless guilt was any lessened by the knowledge there was nothing she could have done to protect them.

Now, what to tell her own people? How can they continue to put their faith in a leader who might not be able to keep them safe from such evil?

Closing her eyes for a moment, Ariana took a deep breath and sat higher in the saddle, trying to ease the painful tension building between her shoulders. The more she searched for a solution to the dark lord problem, the more helpless she felt.

Looking at Alasdair with eyes tinged with worry, Ariana replied, "Of course you are right, Alasdair. My mind knows you are right and yet my heart screams at the injustice as once again it seems Lord Shemar has got away with murder. He taunts me with each evil deed, knowing it will feel like a dagger to my soul while I merely wait for the final thrust to be made."

Alasdair glanced at the defeat in her eyes and knew this was not the leader he had sworn allegiance to. Placing a gloved hand on Aramid's reins, Alasdair said in a low voice, "Please do not think less of me for saying this, milady, but that is your exhaustion speaking. You are thinking the weakness your injury shows you right now is the true nature of Lunadar's leader. I, for one, know this to be false.

I do not believe the gods would allow King Midar to fall to Lord Shemar's dagger just to see his only daughter suffer the same fate. Surely there is something we can do, someone we can turn to who will ally with us to defeat the dark lord!"

The more Ariana listened to Alasdair, the more convinced she became as to the truth found in his counsel.

"Sadly, you are right, Alasdair. There is nothing I could have done to save these people from their fate, but it is still a bitter thing to swallow. I need time to think…time to plan…but time is the one thing of which I have very little.

My ship sails again in one week, and I must be ready to lead it through the portal. If I didn't know better, I would swear there was a spy among us, allowing Lord Shemar to be privy to our every move!"

Glancing once more at the broken bodies lying all around her, Ariana turned Aramid's head toward

Lunadar and said, "Come, Alasdair, let us return home and leave the guards to their work of burying the dead. I am weary in spirit and need a moment of peace to think. I am in no mood to counsel my people today as they require. Tell them their leader still recovers from her injury but will attend to them in the morning. I will go to the sanctuary hall now to seek out the same wisdom my father always found there."

Alasdair looked at Lady Ariana in surprise but wisely kept his thoughts to himself. Giving last minute instructions to the guards, he turned his own horse's head toward Lunadar and urged it into a trot to catch up with the quickly retreating stallion.

CHAPTER THIRTEEN

Ariana's breath seemed to catch in her throat as she paused a moment before placing her hand on the cold brass handle of the door leading to the sanctuary hall. It had been three years since she had been in this room. Just as long since she saw her father die at the hands of the dark lord and she avoided that room until now. Too many ghosts lurked in that hall. Ghosts of fallen comrades and the spirit of her own father as he used to gather his guards around him in wise counsel during the early days of Lunadar.

The idea of a great waterfall city was born in that hall. The news her mother had crossed over and now roamed in paradise with the rest of their ancestors was given to her father in that hall. As long as Ariana could remember, the pulse of Lunadar itself flowed through that hall and she had been avoiding it for the past three years.

She didn't know if it made her appear weak, a coward even in the eyes of her people, but until now Ariana couldn't bring herself to cross that threshold into what she saw as her father's world. She would be the invader, the spy intruding on the memories of a wise king's rulings all born in that hall. Ariana didn't feel worthy of entering her father's domain.

Fighting the weariness settling on her shoulders, Ariana firmly swung the door open and stepped inside. She expected there to be dust everywhere, but the servants had done their duty well. The furniture's dark wood shone from daily polishing, and there was even a small fire burning in the fireplace to chase the chill from the room. Stepping softly across the bear skin rugs scattered across the floor, Ariana slowly made her way to the large desk crouched in the middle of the room like some wild beast waiting to devour her. Craftsmen had spent many weeks lovingly carving this desk for a king they honored and cherished. Now such a gift belonged to her. Would she ever feel worthy of standing before it she wondered?

Easing herself into the large chair, Ariana felt as if her own father's arms were wrapped around her and she took a moment to rest her head against the wood's cool surface. A lone tear escaped when memories came flooding back to her of the times she played at her father's feet as he sat in this very chair. Writing in his journal. Always writing.

As if he raced against Time itself to put down on paper what could not be uttered by word of mouth. How many times had Ariana asked her father what he wrote about? Ten times over the years of her childhood? Ten times ten? But the answer was always the same. "Hush, daughter," King Midar would reply. "These are the dreams of Lunadar's future and the ramblings of an old man. Nothing for you to worry about right now. The time will come when you will rule Lunadar. Then will be the time for you to discover the secrets hidden inside these pages."

Ariana bolted upright in the chair as the memory of her father's words came back to her. *These are the dreams of Lunadar's future...the secrets hidden inside these pages.* What dreams? What secrets? Ariana sat back to look around the room with new eyes. Her father spent many hours in this room writing in his journal. What if those secrets he spoke of could help defend Lunadar against Lord Shemar? What if the dreams of a king could create a world where Candra no longer hid in fear of discovery by those hell-bent on destroying Lunadar's legacy?

Quickly she rummaged through the old maps still lying on the desk but could find no journal among them. A search through the drawers uncovered much the same results. *Father, where have you hidden your secrets?* Ariana closed her eyes once more, trying to recapture the memories of playing in this very room while her father sat here pouring over his papers. The king was a busy man, but never too busy to indulge his offspring with her heart's desire to be near him. *He would have placed such a prized possession somewhere safe. Somewhere no one would think to look except the rightful heir to Lunadar.*

Ariana opened her eyes once more this time to find her mother's eyes staring back at her. A portrait commissioned shortly before her passing hung near a tapestry across the room, and those eyes seemed to be trying to tell Ariana something. *What are you trying to tell me, Mother? Do you know where Father has hidden his journal? Who would have he trusted above all others to keep his secrets?* The more Ariana searched her mother's smiling face, the stronger an idea nibbled at her brain, demanding to be heard. *Could it be the one to hold his heart also held the future of Lunadar hidden behind those smiling eyes?*

Pushing back the chair, Ariana quietly crossed the room and stood in front of her mother's portrait. With trembling hands, she slowly lifted the edge of the portrait to cautiously feel all around until her fingers slid over something wrapped in smooth leather and tucked in the corner of the frame. *Father, I discovered your journal just as you knew I would when you picked this special hiding place!*

Returning to the comfort of her father's chair, Ariana carefully laid the package on the desk before slipping off the ties to reveal the papers stacked neatly inside. Ariana hadn't realized she'd been holding her breath until the sudden whoosh of air escaped her lungs, and she almost felt lightheaded with relief. Some of the pages were yellow with age, and she realized her father must have been keeping his journal for much of his reign. Drawing a candle closer, Ariana recognized her father's strong script as it danced upon the page.

Night of the Winter Solstice:

I wonder if she will be in attendance this night during a time when all lay down their arms to worship the gods and life's good fortune? I cannot believe she does not realize my feelings for her go beyond common courtesy. That a mere glance in my direction would be enough for my heart to be hers forever? No mermaid's song can surely be sweeter than a word falling from those silken lips.

Ariana cheeks felt flushed as she glanced away from the papers in front of her. This was a glimpse into the heart of a king, and she felt like an intruder. Who was this person her father spoke of with words of love? Somehow Ariana knew the mystery woman of the journal wasn't her mother, despite the fact her father loved her mother dearly. So, who was she? Forcing herself to look at her father's journal once more, Ariana read another passage…

Night of the Full Moon

She did not come that night, so I went in search of her. Temperance and duty should have swayed my decision to leave this place, but these invisible ties are stronger than the mind can conceive. In truth, I will conjure a reason for seeking her out. Some malady requiring her assistance or trumped-up whisper of danger on the horizon to spark her interest so that I might share some time in her company without revealing my true reasons for arriving unannounced. I know I run the risk of stepping onto a path I cannot return from, but it is a risk I am willing to take.

Ariana glanced up from the journal to find her mother's eyes still silently watching her. *Did you know of this mystery woman, Mother? A woman who could lure a king away from Lunadar with a mere glance in his direction? Or did you live in ignorance of a heart's betrayal? Just what other secrets did her father keep from them all?*

Closing the journal and tucking it under her arm, Ariana quickly left the sanctuary hall. She'd had enough of ghostly spirits and mysterious moonlit visits for one day. Ariana could also no longer ignore the pain in her shoulder which had been reminding her rest was needed if she was going to be strong enough to stand another Otherworld midnight raid. She would return to her chambers to further study her father's journal. Maybe she would even find a way to save Lunadar from destruction at the hands of Lord Shemar.

For the rest of the day Ariana tried to push any thoughts of her father's journal out of her mind, but it was useless. Even quiet time with Candra before evening meal couldn't prevent the questions swirling in her head. The antics of an energetic three-year-old were certainly entertaining but not distracting enough to keep her from wondering which mystery woman managed to capture the heart of a king.

Finally, after her child was turned over to Macklebee for bedtime rituals, Ariana could turn her attention to the nagging doubts festering all afternoon. Dismissing her lady's maid with a wave of her hand, Ariana sunk into the copper tub filled with lilac scented water and watched the flames dance in the fireplace as a log split in two to shower sparks onto the hearth.

Did her father betray her mother's love, Ariana wondered? It certainly seemed that way if the journal entries were to be believed. Or did he stay the course of his marriage despite these feelings he seemed to have for someone else?

Ariana sunk deeper into the water, oblivious to the overflow as it splashed onto the bearskin rug nearby. The longer she fought to understand this secret side to her father she never knew, the more incensed she became.

How could her father risk his marriage and future happiness to pursue this woman? Had he not shared the sacred vows with her mother? Did he not profess to love her above all others?

Suddenly, without warning, visions of Prince Kaspar came to her. Even without the lure of the mermaid's song, Ariana could feel her heart quicken just at the thought of him. *Why must that water devil invade my thoughts even when he is not around? And why now when I have just discovered my father might have loved another?* Like a devil's advocate, another part of her mind argued back. *Maybe because you wish to be loved like that one day?*

Not wanting to contemplate the weighty truth in that question, Ariana quickly stepped out of the cooling water and wrapped herself in towels warming by the fire.

The flames must be burning brighter than usual this evening, Ariana thought as even her cheeks felt flushed as she made her way to her bed. It couldn't possibly be the prince causing this breathlessness she suddenly felt. Maybe if she searched further through her father's journal, she would put a name to this faceless intruder to her happy childhood memories of her parents. Settling her feather pillow against the bolster, Ariana picked up the leather wrapped journal and turned to another entry.

Attempted a truce meeting with Lord Shemar today but it was of no use. He is determined to destroy all I have long fought to protect and for such an unnecessary reason. We were once like brothers and now his dead eyes look in my direction like he hardly knows me. How was I to know he sought Cordelia's hand in marriage as I did? The gods favored me when she said yes, but no matter how often I confess I knew nothing of his affections for her, the more he insists I won her love by trickery and for that he says I must pay with my life! There is no reasoning with him and already he has begun his reign of terror on my people.

Ariana's breath seemed to catch in her throat as she read the passage. Lord Shemar in love with her mother? Surely this could not be. She always wondered the reason why the dark lord looked down on her family with such hatred. She even asked her father before if he knew why

Lord Shemar hated them so, but it was a topic the king never wanted to discuss and now she knew why. Ariana returned to the pages of the journal and read further.

Is it possible Lord Shemar is in league with Anjou, the henchman of Death? He now has an army of creatures, the likes of which I have never seen. Part wildebeest, part devil, these creatures seek only to do Lord Shemar's bidding as if he had cast some evil spell over them.

Without warning these things he calls Drundles attack our villages and send many a man, woman, or child to an agonizing death with a mere poisonous touch of one of their barbs. They appear fearless and seem to possess superhuman strength. I would fear for the safety of Lunadar itself except for the fact these creatures seem to shy away from the water for some strange reason.

The gods smiled upon me when they brought me to this place. Now, if I can only convince Queen Elysie of the rightness of my mission. Without her help, I fear I will fail at my task to find the Cup of Notari and drive Lord Shemar from this realm forever.

CHAPTER FOURTEEN

Restless dreams filled with dark shadows and water demons stirred Ariana awake hours later. She hadn't even realized she had fallen asleep while reading her father's journal. Macklebee must have come in to bank the fire while she slumbered as she could feel a chill creeping into the now darkened room.

Pulling on her wrap, Ariana stepped onto the balcony to listen to the sounds of the waterfalls near her chambers. The moonlight lit up the castle, and once again Ariana felt a sense of pride in being a part of such a rich heritage as Lunadar offered. But now those very thoughts brought her back to her father and those notes in his journal. Who was that mystery woman? What was the Cup of Notari and how could it defeat the dark lord?

Ariana was so deep in thought it took her a moment to realize the soft whisper of a song running through her mind was beginning to surround her like an embrace. Chill bumps raced up her arms and her heart quickened as she realized there could be only one reason to hear that melody in the very air.

Only one person would come to her in the moonlight when she least expected it. *Will that sea devil never release me from this unwanted bond between us?* Ariana wondered.

But try as she might, she just couldn't muster any feelings of anger as she felt more than saw Prince Kaspar glide through the pools surrounding the castle until he stopped short at her window to gaze up at her with eyes as dark as the night.

She was too tired of the never-ending war with Lord Shemar, too heartsick at her father's possible betrayal to fight the merman quietly watching her every mood. All she wished for was a moment's peace and bowed her head in momentary defeat as she leaned against the balcony railing. Even the prince could tell there was a deep air of sadness about Princess Ariana and he moved closer to her before quietly calling out into the silence surrounding them.

"Good evening, milady. Why do I not find you slumbering at this time of night? You should be resting that shoulder instead of counting away the minutes of moonlight."

Ariana didn't even acknowledge Prince Kaspar's presence other than to say with a catch in her voice, "Why can you not just leave me alone? I am too weary to battle with you right now, you thief of innocence."

Maybe it was the lack of steel in her words. Maybe it was the aura of defeat which lay heavy on her young shoulders. Whatever the reason, Prince Kaspar did not come back with some scathing retort at her name calling as she half expected.

Instead, there was unexpected gentleness in his manner as he replied, "What distresses you so much, milady? Can you not lower that wall you have built around your heart long enough to let another share your burdens? I would gladly do so if you would just allow yourself to think of me as something other than a devil in merman form."

If only she had run into him during the daylight hours. If only she had not discovered her father's journal and the damning secrets found inside. If only she had not been tempted by the moonlight and mermaid's song, maybe Ariana would have been able to silence her tongue. Instead, she finally lifted her head to look into those dark eyes gazing back at her and whispered, "Prince Kaspar, do you know anything about the Cup of Notari?"

For a moment the prince seemed surprised by her question. He hesitated just a moment too long before deciding to answer her, which raised Ariana's suspicions.

"Why yes, Princess Ariana, I have been told the legend of that cup. Why do you ask? Who has been speaking to you about the Cup of Notari, and why does it seem to trouble you so?"

Ariana didn't understand why both her heart and head were suddenly telling her to trust this merman. If it were daylight, she would have easily turned her back on his questions and returned to her chambers. But there was something about the darkness surrounding her that felt right for her. As if the moonlight were challenging her to tell him what was resting so heavily on her heart. Ariana could feel her body give in even as the words flowed from her lips.

"I have found a journal of my father's hidden in the sanctuary hall. His notes speak of the Cup of Notari, but I cannot remember him ever mentioning such a cup to me. What is so special about it?"

Ariana knew Prince Kaspar might suspect there was more behind the question than mere curiosity, but it was the first time she'd allowed him a glimpse into her heart. She was surprised when he didn't push for more. "Well, as a child I was told many stories of magical relics thought to be long lost to this world. One of those relics was the Cup of Notari. Legend has it that whoever possesses the cup can cross the barriers of time and space without the use of a portal."

Ariana looked at Prince Kaspar in disbelief.

"A way to the Otherworld for anyone other than mermaids to cross the realms without having to use the portal? That's impossible!"

"Most people would agree with you, but there are some of the elders who are said to have seen it in action. But I must warn you. If such a cup existed, it comes with a price too high to pay for using it, even for someone as daring as yourself, milady."

"And what price is that, may I ask?"

"Legend has it that the Cup of Notari can only be used by exchanging life for life. One could travel to another place and time but could only return to this world through the sacrifice of someone left behind in the Otherworld."

"Never to be able to return to this world?"

"Never."

"Who could ask such a thing of someone? To turn their back on loved ones or even someone under their protection forever? It would be madness to think anyone would do so willingly."

"Now you can see the power behind owning such a relic. To be able to cast aside one's enemies merely by transporting them to another place and time, then abandoning them there to live out the rest of their lives in exile."

Ariana began to see why her father was so intent on trying to discover the validity of such a relic. She had but one more question for the prince.

"Do you know where the cup was said to have been kept?"

Prince Kaspar stared at Ariana a long moment before answering. The more he gazed at her, the more Ariana was thankful for the shadows which concealed the blush she could feel rising up her neck to stain her cheeks. Glancing away from those piercing eyes, she looked at the waterfalls while she held her breath and waited for his reply. Unknowingly to Ariana, that one hesitation gave away the notion she was hiding something from the prince despite her seemingly casual conversation with him.

"Yes, I know where the legend says the cup resides, but now I wonder why you are curious to know as well? Just what secrets are hidden in that journal of your father's to have you ask such questions of me? Normally you would not lower yourself to even acknowledge my existence!"

Ariana's back stiffened in surprise at how closely he came to identify what lay hidden in the king's journal. Normally a sharp retort would have flown from her lips, but this time she stopped for a moment to think about his words and discovered the truth in what he said.

Quickly replying before her heart might interfere, Ariana said, "My father's journal spoke of using the Cup of Notari to rid this realm of Lord Shemar. As you can see, King Midar failed to accomplish this before the dark lord murdered him!"

"And you wish to complete the pilgrimage first started by the king?"

"Yes."

Prince Kaspar looked at the proud woman standing in front of him, bathed in moonlight and waiting for his answer. Ariana felt certain if anyone could find the Cup of Notari, it would be her. Now if she could just convince him of that.

"Okay, milady, I can tell you what you wish to know but on one condition."

Ariana looked at the cheeky grin beginning to peek out of one corner of the prince's mouth and knew instantly she would not like what she was about to hear.

"What condition?"

"That should you succeed in locating the Cup of Notari, you will allow me to send others on your journey to rid this realm of the dark lord."

"Absolutely not!" Ariana hissed through suddenly clenched teeth.

"Then you will not find the answers you seek, milady!"

"Why you pompous, arrogant sea devil! What makes you think you are the only one to have heard of this legend? I could just as easily find the answers to my question elsewhere!"

The prince's laughter rippled on the wind which just served to anger Ariana even more.

"Oh, you could try, milady, but no one would be able to supply you with the answer you seek. Certain parts of that legend is known only to the people of Renndar and right now you are not the Queen's favorite. I doubt anyone would be willing to risk the wrath of the queen to speak to you."

Again, the moonlight must have whispered caution in Ariana's ear as she took a moment to breathe deeply while trying to ease the tension in her shoulders. The prince could only stare at her in fascination as the different emotions danced across her face.

Finally, Ariana looked at him and replied, "Prince Kaspar, I do not wish to fight with you. I grow weary of this constant tension between us. My father taught me to know my enemy well and to use whatever knowledge I have about them wisely. Since it seems I cannot rid myself of your interference in my life because of that damned mermaid's song, I will accept your condition, but I have one of my own."

Prince Kaspar tilted his head to look at her more closely as he considered her words carefully. "And what would that condition be?"

"That should there ever come a time when someone is forced to take the life of Lord Shemar, you will allow it to be me. I made my father a promise on the battlefield that I would make the dark lord pay dearly for all the suffering he has showered upon Lunadar and its people. It is a promise I intend to keep with or without your help!"

"Agreed, milady."

Ariana thought there would be another test of will between them, so it was rather startling for the prince to give in so easily to her demand. For a moment she was at a loss for words and could only gaze into Prince Kaspar's eyes in surprise. Eyes that began to darken even more before he spoke again.

"I was told the Cup of Notari was last seen somewhere in Quallan Forest. Legend has it that Queen Elysie was going to destroy it so no one would have the chance to use it for evil, but somehow it disappeared before she could complete the task."

"Queen Elysie? She has the cup?"

"So, it would seem if one is to believe the legend."

Ariana closed her eyes for a moment to shut out the prince and think. *Now it made more sense. Queen Elysie told her once her father had come to her rescue to try and recover something important to her. It had to have been the Cup of Notari. But who had taken it? And if her father succeeded in returning the relic to the queen, why is Lord Shemar still here?* She knew the answers to those questions were better found out elsewhere. It was time to visit Queen Elysie again.

Opening her eyes to find the prince staring at her with unanswered questions in his eyes, Ariana gave a slight nod in his direction before deciding to return to her chambers.

"Thank you, Prince Kaspar, for your willingness to answer my questions tonight. It was a surprise and not all too unpleasant experience I might add. We will war again sometime soon, of that I am certain, but for now I will leave you with my gratitude for your help and return to my bed for much needed rest."

Seemingly surprised himself at the outcome of their chance meeting, Prince Kaspar bowed low in the water and called out to Ariana's retreating form, "Sweet dreams, milady. As always, I am yours to command."

Those words came back to haunt Ariana's dreams when she was finally able to fall asleep. But this time, instead of being chased by shadows and sea devils, she found herself surprisingly cradled by unknown arms as she drifted down the pools surrounding Lunadar.

Somehow it did not alarm her to be held in this manner, and when she awoke the next morning her body felt like a great weight had been lifted from it. Ariana wasn't about to question the nature of such a gift, but instead slowly changed into riding clothes and headed in the direction of Quallan Forest. She had much to ask its leader and she hoped the queen was in a talkative mood!

CHAPTER FIFTEEN

Instead of using the forest portal as she had before, Ariana decided this time the direct approach was best. Leaving Alasdair and her guards near the entrance to the forest, Ariana continued the path alone. It seemed like just yesterday she met Queen Elysie for the first time instead of many weeks ago. With her being laid low by her injury, she hadn't even had the chance to thank the queen properly for helping to save her life. *And what about thanking Prince Kaspar?* Her traitorous mind was playing tricks with her again.

Forcing herself to concentrate on the task at hand, Ariana stepped further away from the entrance and felt, more than heard, the wall of vines and shrubbery slowly closing behind her. Glancing around, she could just make out the tree fairies hiding in the foliage as she made her way deeper into the forest. Ariana didn't get far before the silence heralded the approach of someone and to her surprise it was not Queen Elysie who stood before her but her daughter, Tomari. For a moment the two women simply stared at each other before Tomari performed a slight curtsy and spoke with a voice full of curiosity.

"Princess Ariana, to what do we owe the pleasure of your visit to our kingdom?"

Ariana returned the curtsey before replying, "Lady Tomari, thank you for welcoming me to Quallan Forest. I come on a quest of the most importance and seek an audience with Queen Elyse."

"An audience with the queen? I am afraid that is impossible. The queen is meeting with the high council now and cannot be disturbed."

"Is it possible that I might wait for her? I would not ask of this for myself, but it is a matter of life or death to those I hold dear to my heart!"

Tomari silently observed Ariana for a moment before saying, "Life or death did you say? Whose life? Yours?"

Ariana glanced down at the forest floor. "No, the lives of my daughter and my people."

Folding her arms and continuing to stare at the woman standing before her Tomari said, "Exactly what is it you wish from her?"

Ariana debated whether to provide some tale of woe to illicit some sympathy from the queen's daughter, but she quickly realized Tomari would simply see through such a ruse. Far better to align her words as closely to the truth as possible in the hopes no one would uncover the entire reason for her request.

Drawing herself up to her full height, Ariana said, "There is a legend which tells of a way to travel through time and space without the use of a portal. It is said such a relic lies somewhere within Quallan Forest. I wish to discuss the truth of such a relic with Queen Elysie."

Ariana almost missed the flicker of surprise crossing Tomari's face before she replied, "Do you mean to speak of the Cup of Notari? But why would you be interested in the legend? Do you not already travel through the lunar portal yourself to help your people?"

Ariana thought a moment before replying to Tomari's question. Now was the time to decide just how much she could trust the woman standing before her. Normally she would never have considered such a thing but somehow, since that moonlit encounter with Prince Kaspar, Ariana found herself beginning to question the self-induced wall she'd built around herself since her father's death. Maybe the prince was right. Maybe it was time to let someone else see inside, to catch a glimpse of the occasional fear she fought so hard to ignore?

"Milady, I come seeking the queen's council once again because I am tired of this war between Lord Shemar and my people. I'm tired of seeing the children of Lunadar cry themselves to sleep at night because they have lost their parents to the barbs of the Drundles. I am sick of looking into the haunted eyes of my people as they struggle to keep faith in a leader who cannot even manage to put food on their table unless she becomes the thing she despises most.

If the Cup of Notari does exist and Queen Elysie does know of its whereabouts, I beseech you to let me speak to her about it. It is the only way to rid this realm of the evil caused by Lord Shemar's hatred for me simply because I am the daughter of a king!"

Tomari just watched in silence during Ariana's impassioned speech. Once she was through speaking, both women could feel the forest all around them become very quiet. It was as if all the creatures of Quallan Forrest awaited Tomari's response. Finally, the silence was broken when Tomari turned to Ariana and said, "I, too, can feel the pain you must feel for the suffering of your people. Come, take my hand. Follow me and soon you will have the answers you seek, though I am not sure how it will ease your mind."

Gently taking Ariana's hand in her own, Tomari began to take them both deeper into the forest. At first Ariana didn't know where she was but soon, she could tell Tomari was leading her back to Queen Elysie's castle. Ariana's heart quickened as did her pace when she realized she would soon learn where the Cup of Notari was kept hidden. Soon there might be a way to rid Lunadar of the dark lord once and for all!

Low hanging branches were swept aside to reveal the front entrance to the queen's castle. Watching Tomari as she seemed to glide up the stairs and into the grand hallway, Ariana could see much of the queen in the girl.

Born to one day rule Quallan Forest, now all that was needed was a raised eyebrow and Fairie servants hastened to do her bidding. Ariana did not know much about her, but wondered if Tomari might not prove to be a deadly adversary should circumstances ever find them on opposite sides of where they were today.

Soon they came to a doorway leading into a large room and Tomari motioned for Ariana to enter before her. It wasn't until she stepped inside that Ariana realized where she was. Large tapestries hung from the walls and depicted grand battles performed in the service of protecting the people of Quallan Forest. Candle filled sconces illuminated the large, gilded throne located on a high dais at the opposite end of the room. Even the emerald, green carpet and drapes had gold threading woven into the material, causing the whole room to shimmer in the soft candlelight.

Ariana took a moment to look around the room once more before turning to her host. Tomari was watching her very closely as she motioned her to sit upon one of the damask covered benches lining one side of the room. Everywhere Ariana looked, the room spoke to the riches and power of the leader who sat on the throne of Quallan Forest.

Tomari raised an arm to encompass the room and turned to Ariana. "What do you think of our throne room, Princess Ariana?"

Ariana knew she was at a disadvantage, forced to look up at Tomari as the woman glided across the room to stand in a position of power in front of her. Sitting ramrod straight, Ariana looked up into Tomari's eyes and replied, "An elegant and stately room best suited for such a great leader as Queen Elysie."

Tomari seemed pleased with Ariana's response as a small smile tugged at one corner of her mouth. Ariana decided to press once again her reason for coming to Quallan Forest.

"Pray excuse me for asking, but is this where the Cup of Notari is kept?"

In the silence following her question, Ariana suddenly felt a strange energy filling the room before she realized they were no longer alone in the grand throne room. Seeming to materialize from out of nowhere, the soft, lyrical voice of the now seated queen called out to Ariana from where just seconds before the throne stood empty.

"I can see from here the daughter of King Midar seems to have made a full recovery from the injury she sustained at Renndar. I am glad to see you in such fine health."

Ariana sunk to the floor in a low curtsy before rising to stand before the queen.

"I apologize for not being able to come in person sooner to thank you for your assistance in saving my life that day. If not for your intervention, my own daughter would be without her mother right now."

"And Prince Kaspar? Have you thanked him for saving your life as well? For it was he who carried you to safety, not I."

Ariana hoped the queen would not see the sudden flush of her cheeks at the mention of the merman's name and quickly looked away from the throne to gaze at the tapestries before replying in a low voice, "The prince knows the people of Lunadar will always be grateful for his assistance in that matter."

A ghost of a smile appeared on Queen Elysie's face as she watched Ariana's reaction to her question, but all she said was, "And its leader?"

Ariana quickly glanced in the direction of Tomari but was surprised to see they were the only ones left in the room. She had exited the room so quietly Ariana never heard her depart. *So like her mother,* Ariana thought to herself as she turned to look at the queen once more. "I, too, am grateful for Prince Kaspar's help that day." She was very relieved when the queen decided to let the matter drop and chose another topic of discussion instead.

"Who told you about the Cup of Notari and why do you seek to know its whereabouts?"

Ariana felt so close to her vision of ridding Lunadar of the dark lord but knew she had to convince Queen Elysie to share the relic's whereabouts before she could secure Candra's future. She chose her words carefully.

"My father spoke of it before, but it was Prince Kaspar who told me of the legend. Are the whispers true that it is hidden somewhere within Quallan Forest?"

Queen Elyse chose not to answer Ariana's question but posed one of her own.

"What would you do with such a relic should you ever have it within your possession?"

How could she not answer truthfully when she knew the queen could see into the deep recesses of Ariana's heart should she choose to do so?

"I would cast Lord Shemar out of this realm."

The queen's response was immediate. "Even someone as evil as the dark lord has a home. And could your conscience so easily curse him to a life outside the only existence he has ever known?"

There was no hesitation in Ariana's look or manner when she stared directly into Queen Elysie's eyes and replied, "For what Lord Shemar did to my father at the Battle of Roth and the tortuous suffering my people have had to endure at the hands of his Drundles, I would gladly cast him into the Otherworld to live in exile for the rest of his evil days!"

The queen said nothing but continued to stare at Ariana a moment before she waved her hand to magically push aside a velvet curtain not far from where Ariana stood. She turned to see sitting on a small, round table was a tall glass dome covering an open, yet empty wooden chest encrusted with jewels. At first Ariana didn't realize what the queen was trying to show her. Then she knew. Turning back to Queen Elsie with a confused look on her face, Ariana said, "Is that the resting place of the Cup of Notari?"

"Yes."

"But where is the cup now?"

"I am not exactly sure. It was taken from me many years ago. Do you remember the room which honored King Midar's memory?"

"Yes," Ariana replied. "But I do not understand what that has to do…"

"That room honors his attempt to return the relic back to where it belonged. He paid for that attempt with his life."

Ariana shook her head slightly, as if to clear her thoughts, before saying, "The Battle of Roth was started over a relic? And do you mean to say Lord Shemar somehow now possesses the Cup of Notari? But how is that possible?"

Silently gliding over to where Ariana stood by the dome, Queen Elysie reached out to softly touch the cool glass. A soft, hissing sigh escaped her lips as once again she turned to look at Ariana.

"One of my guards was promised many riches from Lord Shemar in exchange for the cup. Foolishly he thought such an evil one as the dark lord would keep his word, but Lord Shemar had no intention of ever paying that guard for what he tricked from me. Your father merely intercepted that guard's midnight ride and sought to retrieve what was rightfully mine. But before he could return the Cup of Notari to me Lord Shemar unleashed the Drundles on Lunadar and your father was thrown into a war not of his own choosing.

Ariana slowly sank back down onto the bench and tried to grasp the scattered thoughts frantically darting around in her head. If what Queen Elsie said was true, then her father paid dearly for a fight that was not even his to champion. Ariana could feel the anger beginning to well up inside her and fought to keep it in check as she glanced up to see the queen watching her every move with great intensity.

No matter how hard she tried to do otherwise, all Ariana could think was the fact she stood in front of the person responsible for her father's death. All this time she thought it was Lord Shemar who was the cause of all her anguish over the loss of a devoted father and the suffering of Lunadar's people.

But in truth, he was only retaliating against the man who stood between him and the relic. It could have been anyone. It should have been Queen Elysie who laid at the end of the dark lord's dagger that day on the battlefield, not her father.

Quickly standing on legs that threatened to buckle beneath her, Ariana looked at Queen Elsie with fearless fury and nearly spat out the words, "You knew my father would possibly die at the Battle of Roth, while not even defending his own people, and still you let him champion you? It should have been you and not my father left to die on that battlefield!"

Ariana realized she had gone too far when the queen's eyes glowed a dark emerald green and began to pulsate with fury until the energy in the room threatened to suffocate her. Reaching out to clutch her arm with talon-like fingers, Queen Elysie jerked Ariana closer and hissed in her ear, "Tread lightly, daughter of King Midar! You forget in whose presence you stand. Your father bowed to no one, and he was no one's fool! You dishonor a great king's memory to think of him as a mere puppet to do my bidding.

He was the one to come to me when he discovered one of my guards had betrayed me. He refused to take back his offer to champion me despite my repeated requests for him to do so. The people of Quallan Forest will forever owe a debt to him for trying to return the Cup of Notari to us. Now leave this place before you discover what I am truly capable of!"

With this, Queen Elysie shoved Ariana away from her in disgust, causing her to tumble against the bench and fall to her knees. Shaking uncontrollably, Ariana hugged herself tightly to stop the trembling. As silently as she had entered the throne room, the queen was gone and all that was left behind was a deafening silence to fill the void.

Slowly Ariana stood up to test the strength of her legs as she wondered if they felt strong enough to support her.

Tomari had returned and stood near the doorway, arms folded across her body as she stared at Ariana with eyes filled with contempt.

There was no use trying to repair the damage she had caused in her haste to judge the queen's actions in the wake of her father's death. All she could do now was depart Quallan Forest as quickly as she could and return to Lunadar to prepare to make another moonlight run to the Otherworld. The problem of Lord Shemar would have to wait until another time.

CHAPTER SIXTEEN

White capped waves broke across the bow as the ship's sails unfurled to meet the westerly winds. It had been three weeks since Ariana's ship slipped through the portal to restock Lunadar's supplies. Another good night's run. The men pushed themselves farther than Ariana had thought possible, and the full storage hold was proof of their efforts. Their mission was complete.

Such a shame the portal wasn't scheduled to open again for a few more days. Ariana glanced at the weariness etched on the faces of her crew and made a quick decision.

"Listen up, men. Your valiant efforts to provide for the people of Lunadar have not gone unnoticed by me. We have more than enough supplies to feed and clothe your children. Now is the time to celebrate another successful voyage with a few days' rest before we return home. Let us set sail for the nearest port!"

The rowdy cheers accompanying her announcement were enough to convince Ariana as to the rightness of her decision. Island life would not solve the problem of Lord Shemar, but if it gave even a moment's peace to her men then that is where they would head.

Shanty's Cove was an old seaport taken over by questionable inhabitants' years before and had many secret inlets to hide a weary sea traveler. Dropping anchor just off the coast, Ariana boarded the skiff to make the short trip to shore. The rest of the crew would take turns partaking of the Island's pleasures. She wasn't about to take any chances of losing that precious cargo after her men had fought so hard to secure it.

After setting up camp quickly, the men went in search of island companionship. For the first time in weeks, Ariana was left to her own devices. The other inhabitants of Shanty's Cove had crossed paths with the standoffish lady pirate before and gave Ariana a wide berth whenever she came to port.

Finishing her meal of fire roasted fish and ale, Ariana headed toward an outcrop of rocks not far from camp. Moonlight made the water shimmer like diamonds and highlighted the antics of otters searching for sea urchins among the kelp beds.

Ariana watched fascinated as a mother otter carefully wrapped her newborn pup in a layer of seaweed to float like a cork as she dove in search of food. *You watch over your child as I do Candra,* she thought to herself. But if the truth were told, Ariana didn't feel like an otter who kept its offspring safe.

She had failed to protect Candra from Queen Naab's guards kidnapping her. Even now Ariana depended on others like Alasdair to protect Lunadar's heir while she rested on some beach in the Otherworld.

The night was as dark as Ariana's thoughts. She hadn't noticed the otter family's departure until the soft strains of the mermaid's song began to float in the air, surrounding Ariana with its melody. Knowing what she would find if she gazed out to sea, she kept her eyes averted until the breeze carried a familiar voice across the rocks to where she sat.

"Good evening, milady. A most glorious night to enjoy the moonlight, don't you agree?" said Prince Kaspar.

Ariana wasn't even surprised to see the merman bobbing in the ocean's surf in front of her. She had come to expect Prince Kaspar's lurking in the shadows of wherever she might venture. And if Ariana were honest with herself, she was even beginning to draw some comfort from that fact, yet she wasn't ready to reveal such a truth to anyone.

"Why must you forever torment me, Prince Kaspar? Why are you here instead of back at Renndar, doing the queen's bidding?"

There was a definite glint in the merman's eyes as he smiled at Ariana and replied, "In case you hadn't realized, milady, you are not the only one who has managed to fall out of favor with my mother."

"Why would Queen Naab find fault with her chosen heir to the throne?"

Prince Kaspar merely stared at Ariana until she realized her faux pas. Of course, Queen Naab would not have been happy to see her saved from harm, but for it to have been her own son to come to Ariana's rescue? That would have only infuriated the sea queen more.

Ariana watched as the prince glided even closer to her. He remained silent, simply staring at her until Ariana felt compelled to say, "Forgive my rudeness, Prince Kaspar. I should have realized it must not have been easy to perform that act of bravery on my behalf. It seems I owe you a debt of gratitude for saving the life of Lunadar's leader."

"I was not thinking of Lunadar or its people when I came to your aid that day, Ariana."

"Oh really, then what were you thinking? For in my mind, it was foolish to put yourself in such danger and now you run the risk of incurring Queen Naab's wrath."

Prince Kaspar pulled himself up onto one of the rocks before turning his full gaze upon Ariana. His voice was low and lyrical as he said, "I did not think it foolish to save the life of my chosen mate, no matter the fact she had invaded my mother's domain to snatch her granddaughter from her."

There it was. The thing Ariana had tried to avoid since the night of the Winter Solstice when Prince Kaspar discovered Candra was of his blood. The moonlight did little to hide her sudden flushed cheeks, and Ariana did the only thing she could think to do to hide the sudden fluttering she felt deep in her stomach. Sitting ramrod straight, she looked down her nose at him. "You mean I rescued my child from possible death if your mother had forced her to go through with the mermaid's test!"

Prince Kaspar's voice took on a steely tone as he replied, "Don't you mean our child? The child you tried to hide from me? Candra has mermaid blood flowing through her veins even if you refuse to acknowledge that fact. It was only fitting she be allowed to endure the test to establish herself as future heir to the throne!"

"Heir to the Renndar throne? Surely you jest. I would never allow such a thing!" Ariana's eyes darkened with fury as she stood to tower over the merman reclining at her feet. Candra was born to rule Lunadar, despite the prince's foolish wishes to the contrary. She half expected him to rebuke her words, so his laughter caught her by surprise.

Resting back on his arms to lean against rocks rubbed smooth by waves, Prince Kaspar laughed again before looking at Ariana with eyes seeming to burn right through her. His voice took on a silky tone as he replied, "Oh, you will allow it, milady, and much more I wager when the time is right. As my wife and future queen of Renndar, it is only fitting our child should be schooled in the ways of the mermaids."

Ariana stared at the merman as if he'd turned into a dangerous sea serpent before her very eyes. Be his wife? Surely the moon had made him mad!

"Have you lost hold of your senses? Me become your wife? Poseidon himself could unleash the Kraken upon Lunadar and still I would not lower myself to unite with a sea devil like you!"

Ariana wanted to throw something at him as Prince Kaspar only laughed again before sliding back into the waves. "Save your barbed tongue for Lord Shemar, milady. Fight the call of the mermaid's song all you want but, in the end, you will be my woman and sit next to me on the throne of Renndar. Now that I know I have an heir, I am more certain than ever of that fact. I will give you time to come to the realization the gods have entwined our futures, but do not test my patience for long or you will surely suffer the consequences for such rash behavior!"

His words continued to echo on the wind long after he disappeared beneath the foamy waves. Ariana could only stare speechlessly at the dark water in surprise. How dare that arrogant sea devil think she would ever consent to become his wife? And to think she was even beginning to enjoy his company. Any peace she thought of finding on Shanty's Cove was ruined, and Ariana couldn't wait to return to Lunadar, so she could put Prince Kaspar out of her mind once and for all!

CHAPTER SEVENTEEN

The ship crawled silently through the maze of rocks as Ariana turned the bow toward home. Waiting for the portal to open was a lesson in frustration as she could not get Prince Kaspar's words out of her head. The men took full advantage of the island's pleasures, but Ariana remained secluded at their camp, resting fitfully until she welcomed being able to return to the ship.

Once aboard, she gave such sharp commands to hasten the sails the men ran to do her bidding. Ariana knew she was driving the men mercilessly, but the restlessness inside her would not be stilled, and she prayed peace would return to her once they were back upon the solid ground of Lunadar's shores.

A few more turns of the wheel and the ship slipped through the portal just as it was beginning to close. Another clean run, not a life lost, and soon they would be back in the arms of loved ones. What more could Ariana ask of the gods?

Someone with which to share this burden and lighten the yoke of responsibility?

Unbidden, the thought crossed her mind as she noticed dolphins skimming the water beside the ship as if to challenge it to a race. *Oh, to have the freedom to follow wherever the waves take you,* Ariana thought as she turned the ship in the direction of Dreydan's Falls. Just one more nautical mile and they would be pulling into port.

Just a little more time and Ariana could hold Candra once more. It was getting harder to leave her each time, fearful of what might happen while she was away. Ever since Renndar, Ariana felt on edge. Nothing could shake the feeling of something evil hiding in the shadow, determined to steal her happiness and the future of Lunadar.

The sudden cracking sound of wood splintering as a cannonball careened off the starboard bow startled Ariana out of her reverie and she spun in the direction of the noise. Men scrambled to their battle stations from down below as more cannon fire split the silence of the predawn world they had just slipped into. Ariana's eyes strained to make out the flag of the ship quickly gaining on them.

Suddenly she knew who was attacking them. The telltale flag of devil's fire and crossbones could mean only one thing. It wasn't often the dark lord took to the seas, but today Lord Shemar hid in the shadows of the cliffs leading to her secret cove until he could ambush Ariana on her return home. If he managed to overtake them, his evil crew would cause much damage to her ship and Lunadar's provisions. She could not let that happen.

Quickly shouting orders for her men to return fire, Ariana mentally made some quick calculations. During the daylight hours, the waterfalls and cliffs making up Dreydan's Falls can challenge even the most seasoned sailor. To the unexperienced, those choppy waters can trick a ship to skirt too close to the cliffs' edge until it was too late, and the ship is doomed to slip into the dark abyss lurking below one side of the waterfalls.

If she timed it just right, they could outrun Lord Shemar while avoiding being trapped between his ship and the edge of the falls. Pulling hard on the wheel, Ariana turned her ship parallel to the waterfalls and prayed the gods would have mercy on them that night.

Looking over her shoulder, at first Ariana wondered why there was no longer cannon fire coming from the other ship. Suddenly she realized how foolish she had become in her haste to get away from the dark lord. He wasn't interested in doing battle on the seas. The only reason he released the cannonballs on her ship was to push her toward Dreydan's Falls and let the deadly waters do the rest. What a fool she was not to have seen his motives before now!

Gripping the steering wheel even tighter in her hands, Ariana shouted out more commands for every available body to man the oars. No longer could they just rely on the wind to save them. Every man now needed to row with every ounce of strength he possessed. As if his very life depended on it, for in truth, it did.

The roar of the waterfalls thundered in her ears and the spray lashed her face as the pull of the current steered the ship closer to the rocky edge of the abyss. Ariana's men strained against the oars as they fought the sea. The wheel became a wild, bucking beast beneath her hands as she fought for control. It would be so easy to let go and release her spirit to the sea; to let the water carry her over the edge and to know Lord Shemar would win.

She was tired of this fight she did not ask for. She could wish for the chance to cast aside this heavy cloak of responsibility and let the sea take her where it will. But her men needed her. They depended on her guidance to lead them safely home. Even more than her men, Candra needed a mother, even a damaged one, to steer her through the treacherous waters of childhood. Much like the churning, foaming waters she strained to overcome.

Crying out to the gods, she tightened her grip on the wheel once more and renewed her fight with the beast beneath her hands. The wood cut deep into her palms as she gripped the wheel with both hands. Slowly, inch by inch, she felt the ship shutter as it strained to regain its bearings, and it began to slip away from the cliffs. She breathed a sigh of relief as she could finally turn the ship toward Lunadar and leave the waterfalls behind.

It wasn't until later that Ariana stepped inside her bedchambers and closed the door behind her when she allowed herself to think about what had just happened. Digging nails into the soft flesh of her already injured palms, Ariana barely made it to her bedside before the trembling began as she faced the reality her whole crew might have died that night due to her negligence.

Wives and children might have screamed at the injustice if the gods had chosen a different outcome. Looking down at her hands, Ariana sought to still their trembling by wrapping her arms tightly around herself.

What is happening to me? She wondered. *I used to be a fierce fighter, defending the legacy of Lunadar without hesitation, but tonight I let the words of some sea devil distract me to the point my men almost perished! What kind of person am I to have almost left Candra without a mother's love to cherish and guide her?*

Self-doubt crowded all around her, suffocating her until she ran from the room to stand on her balcony and drink in the calming, moonlit air. Ariana didn't notice at first the prince watching quietly from the shadows, never heard the soft melody riding in on the evening breeze until Prince Kaspar called out to her, "Milady, what is wrong? What has happened to cause you such anguish?"

Startled, Ariana turned to stare into eyes as dark as the shadows he came from and filled with concern as he watched her every move. The last person she wanted to encounter when she felt like this was him. She feared Prince Kaspar would take full advantage of any display of weakness if he could. Hiding her still trembling hands behind her, Ariana drew her shoulders taunt before addressing the merman.

"There is nothing wrong, Prince Kaspar. The moonlight has played tricks on your eyes. And might I ask why you have invaded Lunadar's grounds once more without so much as a please to its leader?"

Prince Kaspar glided even closer to the balcony while staring intently at her for another moment before replying, "You cannot fool me with mock bravado, Ariana. I know your every mood as well as I know the creatures of the sea, and something has upset you greatly. I wish to know what has happened to cause you to hide your trembling hands from my view. You are many things, Ariana, but coy is not one of your virtues. Pray, be honest with me now!"

Ariana quickly realized it was no use to continue this cat and mouse game with Prince Kaspar. He would never give her a moment's peace until he uncovered the truth of what happened tonight. Far better to try and minimize the severity of the encounter with the dark lord and pray it satisfies the sea devil's curiosity. Closing her eyes while drawing more cooling air into her lungs, Ariana finally looked at the prince and said, "It was of no consequence. My men and I merely ran into Lord Shemar on our way home, and it was a most unpleasant encounter as usual."

Prince Kaspar didn't say a word but continued to stare at Ariana until she broke eye contact with him. That was all he needed to inspire him to ask one question.

"Where?"

Taking a step backwards, further into the shadows, Ariana replied, "Where what?"

A small frown tugged at the corner of the prince's mouth. Eyes the color of a stormy sea held her captive as he said, "Exactly where might you and your men have run into Lord Shemar? Answer me, Ariana!"

Startled the prince chose then to take such a tone with her, Ariana uttered the words she swore not to tell him.

"Dreydan's Falls."

"Dreydan's Falls? But those currents are dangerous to travel through, no matter the time! What happened?"

Ariana knew it was no use delaying the outcome of their heated discussion. Prince Kaspar would continue to force his will upon her in his search for answers, and she was bone weary with exhaustion. Dropping her shoulders in defeat, Ariana hugged her middle and replied in a low voice suddenly full of tears, "I was foolishly distracted but a moment and the dark lord caught me unawares. Lord Shemar attempted to drive us over the waterfalls, but we managed to turn the ship away just in time. It is over now and best forgotten."

Prince Kaspar took one look at the figure silhouetted by the moonlight and all anger vanished as concerned colored his next words. "It must have been terrifying for you, Ariana. You always run an excellent ship, but no doubt you were more concerned for the safety of your men as well as young Candra, rather than yourself."

Ariana looked at the prince through misty eyes and wondered who was this creature in front of her? When did he go from being a sea devil sent to torment her to this now seductive man of reason and concern for her wellbeing? It made no sense, and Ariana was too drained of energy to fight her emotions. If she didn't leave now, she feared she would embarrass herself in front of Prince Kaspar by crying.

Stepping further into the shadows, Ariana replied, "As I said, it is of no consequence. I am very tired, Prince Kaspar, so I'm sure you will forgive me if I retire now. It has been a long day, and I must rest so I can make plans in the morning on how I will deal with the dark lord's latest treachery. I bid you good night."

Prince Kaspar rose above the waters until he was almost eye level with Ariana and said in a soft, hypnotic voice, "Sweet dreams, my fair lady. Do not doubt the wisdom of your ability to lead your people, just as you should not doubt the sincerity of my devotion to fulfilling your smallest desire."

With a small bow in her direction, the prince turned and sank beneath the waves before Ariana could even think of a way to respond to such words. Making her way slowly to her bed, Ariana soon fell into a deep sleep to dream of dark, dancing eyes daring her to follow as she swayed to the echoes of the mermaid's song.

CHAPTER EIGHTEEN

Ariana peeked out from under her bed covers the next morning to see Macklebee pulling back the heavy tapestry curtains to let the sunlight into her bed chambers. Squeals of childish laughter accompanied a small bundle of energy as Candra climbed up to snuggle next to her mother in the feather bed.

Taking a moment to plant a kiss on her daughter's shining black hair, Ariana breathed in the smell of rose petals Candra bathed in the previous night, and a small sigh escaped her lips. Macklebee turned at the sound and watched the two figures on the bed a moment before saying, "Good morning, milady. I trust you had a restful night. 'Tis a beautiful day to behold and one you will wish to see for yourself, no doubt."

Ariana gave Candra one last hug and kiss before sending her daughter back to the nursery for breakfast with her nanny. Drawing her wrap closely to her, Ariana sighed again and looked at the morning light dancing off the waterfalls near her window before asking her manservant the question hovering on her mind since the encounter with Lord Shemar at Dreydan's Falls.

"Macklebee, I have a question to ask, and I expect nothing but the truth from you."

Macklebee turned to glance at Ariana with a confused look in his eyes before saying, "But of course, Princess Ariana. You may always depend on the utmost honesty from me."

Ariana sighed once more and said in a voice Macklebee had to lean closer to hear.

"Macklebee, am I a terrible mother?"

The shock could be heard in his voice as Macklebee exclaimed, "A terrible mother? Who dares to say such a thing about you, milady? Why, a more loving, devoted mother isn't to be found in the whole of Lunadar!"

Ariana almost smiled at his words. Such blind devotion to another was seldom found any more. She knew her father would have been proud of the fact Macklebee chose to continue serving Lunadar and its current leader in such a manner.

"Oh, Macklebee, I am truly touched by your words, but I wonder if you are looking at your leader through rose-colored glasses. Try as I might, I fear I have failed miserably in both my duties to Lunadar and to my duties as mother to the future heir of this realm."

Macklebee stepped closer to Ariana and said in a voice filled with concern, "Princess Ariana, why do you now question yourself in such a manner? What has happened to place you on this path of self-doubt?"

Without going into detail, Ariana quickly told Macklebee about her encounter with Lord Shemar, skimming over the fact she and her crew almost fell to their death. No need to distress him over a course which never came to be. When she was finished, Ariana walked out on the balcony to stare at the churning waters beneath her.

Following her, Macklebee timidly placed his hand on the sleeve of Ariana's wrap and said, "Milady, you cannot take one moment in time and allow it to color your judgement of all that you have accomplished since your father's passing. Why, the people of Lunadar would starve if it were not for you and your moonlight raids. And as far as your daughter is concerned, there could be no better mother the gods could have chosen for her."

Ariana turned to Macklebee with a catch in her voice and said, "But don't you see, Macklebee? It wasn't the gods who chose me to be Candra's mother. It was that sea devil and his curse of a mermaid's song!" Tears sprung to her eyes at the mere thought of Prince Kaspar, and Ariana turned away from her manservant to stare at the waterfalls through misty eyes. It was so hard not to despise the prince for the trickery played on her so long ago, but how could she harbor such animosity toward the very person who helped create her beautiful daughter? She hung her head and whispered, "How much longer will I be able to fight this invisible bondage he has over me? Try as I might, I find it becoming harder to resist what trembles between us every time he approaches me."

Macklebee gently laid his hand on Ariana's arm once more and replied, "Please forgive an old servant's words, milady, but is it the trickery of Prince Kaspar's deed which troubles you so, or the fact you may have grown quite used to his company? Perchance, one day, you might even grow fond of his courtly advances?"

Startled out of her inward thoughts by Macklebee's words, Ariana spun around to stare at him. "Me? Care for the prince? Never! He is merely a thorn in my side to be tolerated until I can decipher a way to break the spell his mermaid's song has over me. We will speak no more of this. I must ready myself for my war counsel with Alasdair so tell my lady's maid to attend me!"

Macklebee wisely kept his lips closed and hurried to do as his leader commanded. But the silence left behind his departure did not silence the questions in Ariana's mind from nagging at her as she waited for her lady's maid to come to her.

What is it that you truly feel for Prince Kaspar? When did the loathing for the mere sight of him turn into this catch in your throat whenever he comes into view? And when did he change from the heartless sea devil to the kind, fierce protector who, in all honesty, has come to your rescue not once but twice without you even bothering to thank him for saving your life?

Ariana knew she would have to face those nagging questions one day soon, but for now she forcibly pushed those uneasy thoughts from her mind and quickly dressed for her meeting with the captain of her guards. Without help and guidance from Queen Elysie it was going to be difficult, if not impossible, to attempt to recover the Cup of Notari from the dark lord. Ariana could see no other recourse but to begin a quest to uncover where Lord Shemar hid the ancient relic and secured it for the future of Lunadar.

Later, it felt strange stepping into the sanctuary hall to discuss this mission with Alasdair, but Ariana wanted to feel her father's presence as they planned how to search for the Cup of Notari.

Crossing the room to lay the journal she carried on the desk, Ariana untied the well-worn leather straps and sat down to read further. Maybe there would be a clue within those pages to tell her where the relic was hidden.

How many hours have I sat in the room beating my head against this wall I cannot seem to get around? Such high hopes had I when I first told Queen Elysie I would return the cup of Notari to its rightful owner. Oh, how I crowed that one such as I could never fail in this quest! But the gods do not suffer fools gladly and their displeasure over a king's boastfulness was quickly revealed to me. No matter the plans I made or the commands I gave the captain of my guards, the Drundles made small work of my men. They fell like leaves covering the forest floor before a Winter's Solstice. What a blow to a king's pride to be forced to call a retreat before such evil. But return to Lunadar I must. To carry the shame of my actions as well as words of sorrow to the families of those who fell on the field of battle while defending their king.

Time now to recover from our losses and plan again how to recover the Cup of Notari. Such magic in the hands of such evil can only mean utter destruction for the peoples of Lunadar and possibly even Quallan Forest. Lord Shemar has been driven mad by this jealousy over my marriage to Cordelia. I must find a way to enter his castle beyond Tumac Mountain and safeguard Ariana's future while proving myself worthy of another. May the gods see the rightness of this mission and bless this quest!

Ariana looked up from the journal pages to see Alasdair standing in the doorway. Retying the leather straps before motioning him to enter, she looked at him through new eyes. Alasdair served her father for many years, nearly as many as Macklebee had served the king. Based on what she had just read, Ariana was sure it was Alasdair who was by King Midar's side when the dark lord fought them for control of the relic. How did he manage to escape the Drundles she wondered? It was a question to which she very much wanted an answer.

Noticing Ariana staring at him in a strange manner, Alasdair hesitated in the doorway and cautiously said, "Is everything all right, milady?"

Ariana moved from behind the desk and motioned for him to sit before answering, "Yes, Alasdair, but I have discovered something of great import I wish to discuss with you privately."

"A discovery? I am intrigued. Please share your concerns, Princess Ariana, as I am yours to command."

Ariana stepped across the room to sit in a straight-backed chair opposite Alasdair. Folding her hands carefully in front of her, Ariana looked directly at the captain of her guards and said, "Did you know my father kept a journal of important events during his reign over Lunadar?"

"A journal, milady? I'm afraid I was not privy to such information."

"Such a journal is now in my possession, and I have been studying its contents. He talks about a magical relic called the Cup of Notari. Have you heard of such a relic, Alasdair?"

She heard the sharp intake of breath and saw the surprise in Alasdair's eyes he tried to hide before he replied, "Why yes, milady, I've heard of such a relic. Why do you ask me such a question?"

"My father wrote about the Cup of Notari being taken from Quallan Forest. He even writes about a battle to attempt to recover the relic, but his quest failed. Would you know anything about such a quest, Alasdair?"

The captain rubbed his eyes as if to give him time to compose himself before calmly saying, "Yes, milady, I know of such a quest."

Ariana unclenched her hands and realized she had been holding her breath while she awaited his reply.

Nervously smoothing the velvet of her dress, Ariana said, "Pray tell me of this battle. My father speaks of many deaths because of the Drundles. Were you the captain of the guards then? Surely you would have perished with the rest of the guards so how is it you sit before me if you served my father then?"

Alasdair hung his head and replied in a voice raw with emotion, "Yes, Princess Ariana, I accompanied King Midar on his quest to return the Cup of Notari to Quallan Forest. I will remember that terrible day until I pass from this realm."

"We secretly followed Lord Shemar back to his castle just beyond Tumac Mountain, hoping to engage him in a surprise attack. Every man knew of the immense danger waiting for us with his Drundles lurking in the shadows, but everyone to the last man pledged his allegiance to the king."

Ariana could see how much of a strain this was placing on Alasdair, but she had to know what happened if they were to have any chance of avoiding repeating history. She remained quiet as he continued his story.

"We almost breached the castle compound when the Drundles seemed to surround us from all directions at once. It was if they knew we were coming."

"They knew you were coming?"

"I could never be certain, but I would be willing to bet Lord Shemar not only knew of our intentions but had time to plan a counterattack!"

"But who would do such a thing? Surely not anyone in Lunadar!"

"As I say, milady, we could never discover if someone announced our arrival beforehand. All I know is that many died that day. Too many, and we were unsuccessful in returning the Cup of Notari to Quallan Forest."

Ariana knew there was one more question she had to ask him.

"Alasdair, if you were the captain of my father's guards, then how did you manage to avoid the Drundles' deadly barbs?"

"That is a question I have asked myself every day since then, milady, but have no answer to give you. The king was forced to call a retreat, and we raced back to Dreydan's Falls. Some of the Drundles pursued us and those foolish enough to get too close to the waters paid a most terrible price for choosing to do the dark lord's bidding."

"And the Cup of Notari?"

"Lord Shemar still controls the relic. Why do you ask these questions of me, milady?"

Ariana glanced over to the desk where her father's journal lay. *Father, is this madness to attempt to complete your quest to return the Cup of Notari to Quallan Forest? I look to your spirit to show me the way to achieve this in your honor.*

Ariana closed her eyes for a moment, hoping the answers to her questions could be found within those four walls, but only the stillness echoed back to her. Opening her eyes to find Alasdair patiently watching her, Ariana gave a small sigh before quietly stating, "I plan on going after the relic."

Alasdair blinked in surprise. "But, milady, why? Have not enough died from such an attempt?"

"Alasdair, my father seemed to think this realm needed rid of evil such as the dark lord possesses. Now Lord Shemar controls the Cup of Notari where he can destroy anyone he likes with a mere wave of his hand. Queen Elysie even sought to destroy the relic before Lord Shemar spirited it away from her keeping. How can I stand around to watch the people and places I love to be destroyed just because I fear the outcome of attempting such a quest? Do not the people of Lunadar expect their leader to be fierce in protecting them?"

"Milady, you have always been wise beyond your years, but this time I beseech you to reconsider attempting such a task. I was there. I saw the carnage. I know what the Drundles can do, especially in the safety of their own homeland. It would be suicide!"

"Should I ask you to lead my men on such a quest, would you refuse me?"

"Milady! Why would you ever think such a thing! I am yours to command. I am not afraid to serve Lunadar, even with my life, but I do not believe a wise leader would deliberately send their men into certain death."

"So, you think me unwise?"

"I think you wish to honor King Midar. I believe you wish to end the reign of terror Lord Shemar has showered on the people of Lunadar. And I think you believe the Cup of Notari will help you achieve that purpose."

"And you disagree?"

Alasdair took a moment to consider the question before replying, "In truth, milady, I'm at a loss at how to defeat Lord Shemar and his Drundles. Despite our best efforts, they overcome us at every opportunity. The people of Lunadar barely exist now as it is and would certainly perish if it were not for your moonlit raids. This war between our two realms has gone on far too long, and yet I see no end in sight."

"I understand your concerns, Alasdair. I lie awake at night considering the same thing and sometimes wonder if Lunadar would not be better off with a different leader."

Alasdair looked at Ariana in surprise. "Surely you don't truthfully believe that? King Midar was a great leader and his daughter inherited many of those same qualities. You are but young in your role as Lunadar's leader, but I see no fault in how you have championed your people so far."

"You are right, Alasdair. I am young. Maybe too young to think I can challenge someone like Lord Shemar. Someone older and wiser like my father might have done things differently were he still here."

"I choose not to look to the past but gaze at the future, and the future of Lunadar lay with you, milady. You and your daughter are the future of this realm and if your people did not believe you were strong enough to lead them, despite your youth, there would have been revolts before now. If everyone around you chooses to have faith in your ability to lead, how is it you have so little of it yourself?"

Ariana stood to consider the truth of Alasdair's words and motioned for him to rise before her. She had come to sanctuary hall in search of her father's guidance. She thought she had lost him when his words didn't whisper to her during the silence. But maybe she was looking in the wrong direction? The gods seem to have chosen to answer her questions of doubt in her own abilities with the wisdom of the man sitting before her. Should she not accept such a gift and act upon it?

Nodding briefly to Alasdair, Ariana said, "Thank you for your words of truth and wisdom Alasdair. My father taught me well in the ways of ruling Lunadar, and I dishonor his memory by allowing my own childish fears to stand in the way of what is right.

This reign of evil has gone on far too long. I must do everything in my power to stop it for the sake of my own daughter and the future of Lunadar. We will mount a campaign in two weeks' time to honor the king's wishes and return the Cup of Notari to its rightful owner or perish in our quest. Ready the men for such a mission and may the gods favor a safe return for us all!"

Alasdair bowed before leaving the room to fulfill her orders. Ariana turned to look at her mother's face smiling back at her.

Oh Mother, I hope I have chosen the correct path. I fear I have placed Candra's future in the hands of the dark lord, but what other course could I have chosen? I know in my heart that if I do not act now, it is only a matter of time before Lord Shemar and his Drundles lay waste to everything and everyone I hold dear. What choice do I have but to complete this quest and hope I have not consigned my precious daughter to a life without her mother?

Ariana's questions were only met with silence. Glancing around the room once more, she scooped up her father's journal to return to her chambers. There was much to plan if they were to have a chance of success and very little time in which to do it!

CHAPTER NINETEEN

Hours later Ariana stepped out of the tub, allowing her lady's maid to place a towel around her and begin to brush one hundred strokes through her jet-black hair. If the maid wondered why there were now two streaks of white running through her tresses, she kept her own council. Besides, what could Ariana have told her?

Her people had an inkling as to what their leader was forced to do to keep them from starving, but why should they also worry if the use of her mystic powers to save them is also draining the very life from her with every use? The other servants had long retired to their chambers and even Candra slumbered in her room. Ariana, however, was wide awake and restless. She and Alasdair, along with the rest of her guards, had gone through every painstaking detail of their quest to return the Cup of Notari to Quallan Forest.

Two groups, one led by Alasdair and the other by Ariana herself, would strike out for Tumac Mountain in three days' time to hopefully divert the Drundles away from Lord Shemar's castle to pursue one of the regiments retreating to Dreydan's Falls. The other regiment would then continue to the dark lord's castle to search for the relic.

A dangerously risky venture to be sure, but what other choice did they have? Power such as could be found in the Cup of Notari did not belong in the hands of evil. King Midar and Queen Elysie knew that, and Ariana would do everything within her power to make sure Lord Shemar would not have a chance to use such power to destroy Lunadar.

Finally dismissing her maid with a wave of her hand, Ariana began to pace the floor of her chambers. No matter how much she tried, she was still unable to capture a moment's peace from the day's battle plans running through in her mind. Was she insane to consign her men to such a dangerous task? It was very likely that by this time next week quite a few of them or even herself would meet a tortuous death at the tip of a Drundles' barb. Could she in good faith ask such a sacrifice of them?

Reaching for her wrap, Ariana stepped onto her balcony in search of some peace. Closing her eyes to the starless night, she heard a nightingale as it sang its full-throated song from somewhere beyond the waterfalls. But soon another song could be heard. Low at first, then growing louder, it snaked itself around Ariana until she felt her body move to the melody as if it had a mind of its own.

The mermaid's song.

She should have known he was out there, waiting for her. Ariana had not seen or heard from Prince Kaspar since last night and yet, in her heart, she knew he still lingered not far from her side. She knew she should turn him away from Lunadar and insist he return to his own home, but if she dared admit it to herself, a small part of her would rather he linger nearby.

Gripping the edge of the balcony to force her body to stop its swaying, Ariana looked in the direction she knew Prince Kaspar would appear. As if on cue, the prince rose from the surf like some sea god and stopped beneath her balcony to look up at her.

"Now I understand why the stars have hidden themselves in shame this night. They know they cannot compare to the beauty of your face, Ariana."

Ariana looked into those sea green eyes she was beginning to know so well and raised one eyebrow. "Oh, save such romantic dribble for the silly females of Renndar who choose to worship at your feet. I do not have time for such foolishness."

"Worship at my feet, you say? Well, in case you haven't noticed, milady, I don't normally possess such a human attachment as feet," Prince Kaspar replied with a smile.

For a moment Ariana was at a loss for words, and she could feel the beginning of a blush sneaking into her cheeks. Quickly she countered, "You know very well what I mean. If you are here to banter sweet words around, you would be better served to return to the waters from which you came."

Prince Kaspar rose higher in the waves to stare at her. Ariana could feel the tension in the night air beginning to pulsate around her as his voice took on a silkiness she knew she should steel her heart against, but somehow she didn't attempt to resist.

"Oh, but I so enjoy bantering around those 'sweet words' as you call them, especially when I can shower them on my chosen one."

Ariana tried to stir up some anger at his words, but that voice was beginning to become like a drug to her, and she could only reply weakly, "Why do you continue to insist there will ever be anything more between us than that one night? I will never be yours, no matter how much you might wish it so."

"That is where you are mistaken, milady. Try as you might, there is no denying the pull of the mermaid's song. Even now I can see it calls to you. The blush you try to hide, and the swaying of your body I saw earlier tells a different story. You may deny it all you wish, Ariana, but the signs say otherwise. It is only a matter of time before you will come to me."

Ariana could only stare at the merman in shock. She wanted to summon a scathing retort to say to him, but something stopped her. Butterflies began to dance around inside her. *Dear gods! What if what he says is true? What if some part of me is succumbing to his spell? It simply cannot be so!*

Ariana looked down in confusion at her hands as the prince waited in silence for her reply. When she finally looked back into his eyes, there was a touch of fear lingering in them that seemed to surprise him. Gliding closer, Prince Kaspar rode on the swell of the incoming tide to raise himself to his full height before reaching out to gently cover her hands with his own. Softly he whispered, "Would it really be such a terrible thing to imagine a future with me by your side, Ariana?"

Ariana watched in fascination as those sea green eyes began to change color, swirling into a deep blue which seemed to glow from somewhere deep inside the prince. She knew she should slip her hands from his embrace, but the warmth she felt ever since he first touched her seemed to be gliding up her arms, caressing her, until she knew just seconds before it happened that the prince intended to kiss her.

His lips were cool at first and tasted like the sea. Ariana's eyes fluttered close and a soft sigh escaped her lips as she felt the prince draw her closer to him. Her mind kept telling her to stop this madness, but her lips were clinging to his like she was drowning, and he was her only lifeline.

After what seemed like an eternity, Prince Kaspar slowly retreated, breaking contact, and watched in silence as Ariana could only stare at him with a dazed look in her eyes. A slow, satisfied smile tugged at the corner of his mouth as he said, "Choose whatever words you may, Ariana, to deny what is between us but your lips have just told me otherwise. You know in your own heart that you are already mine, so why do you insist on continuing this war between us?"

Ariana clenched her hands by her side and stared at the prince. "Do not flatter yourself, Prince Kaspar, by what just transpired between us. A mere kiss doesn't betroth me to you, and there is no war between us. The only war I plan to wage is the one with Lord Shemar in three days' time!"

As soon as the words left her lips, Ariana wished she could snatch them back. She had not intended to speak of her plans to march on the dark lord's castle to him, and Ariana could tell by the stiffening of the merman's posture that he would have issue with her words.

Prince Kaspar's eyes narrowed as he said, "Just what do you mean that you plan to wage a war on Lord Shemar in three days' time?"

Ariana's mind raced as she tried to think of some way to keep the prince from learning of her plans. Seeing her begin to fidget, steel crept into his voice as Prince Kaspar said again, "Ariana, just what are your plans in three days' time? I insist you answer me!"

Ariana's chin rose as she stopped to look down at him. "Who are you to tell me that you insist on an answer from me? You are speaking to the leader of Lunadar, not some wench from your castle!"

Prince Kaspar's eyes seem to flash fire as he retorted, "And I am not some flunky for you to bandy about. I am the heir to Renndar, and you will tell me what you are trying to hide from me, or I promise you, milady, you will suffer the consequences of your foolishness for denying me the answer to my question!"

Ariana didn't know if it was the steel she heard in his voice or his overbearing manner, but for a second fear flashed through her body, and she hesitated in refusing him. Oh, what did it matter if she told him of her plans? He would learn soon enough. Breaking eye contact with the merman, Ariana looked to the waterfalls and said, "In three days' time my men and I go on a quest to return the Cup of Notari to its rightful owner."

"You intend to do what?" Prince Kaspar roared. "Have you loss charge of your senses, woman? Do you even know where the relic is being kept?"

"Yes, of course I know. Lord Shemar holds it at his castle."

"And Queen Elysie knows of this folly?"

"Queen Elysie does not rule over Lunadar nor its leader. She has no say so in this matter."

"That fact may be true, Ariana, but she does know what it is like to go up against the dark lord's Drundles and fail. Your own father attempted such foolishness and lost nearly all his men in the process. Do you care so little for your people that you would deliberately call them into harm's way to serve your own childish ideas of a successful outcome?"

"Of course, I care for my men! But pray tell, what would you have me do? Lie around like some spineless creature and just let that evil beast destroy Lunadar without lifting a finger to stop him? Stand around and watch as he takes Candra's future place as heir to this realm? Can't you see if there was any other way to stop this insanity, I would gladly choose another path? Prince Kaspar, my people can no longer stand around and watch their children perish from hunger or die from the prick of a Drundle's barb.

"You have seen for yourself how dangerous it is for me to sail in the Otherworld. My life was spared due only to your own interference when that warship sought to capture me and my men. It is only a matter of time before I am caught and hung for the pirate I am forced to become.

At least if I go on this quest, I challenge the gods to allow me to rule Lunadar on my own terms. To be the leader my people need me to be. Should I perish on this journey, at least they will know I fought in their honor and never succumbed to fear!"

Prince Kaspar said nothing at first, simply staring at her when she finally turned to look at him. It took all her inner strength not to look away. She could sense the anger draining from the prince as he slowly lowered himself back into the sea and quietly said, "Your people do right by Lunadar to follow such a fearless leader. While I see the wisdom in your decision to force Lord Shemar's hand in battle, I fear this quest will not have the outcome you desire. I wish to offer my protection for you and your men. My water sprites might be of some service to your cause should the need arise."

"Prince Kaspar, while I am grateful for such a generous offer, I cannot in good conscience accept such assistance from you. My men are fully versed in the possible danger involved in following their leader into this battle, but it is Lunadar's war with the dark lord, not Renndar's."

Prince Kaspar ran his hand through his hair in frustration. "Ariana, I am aware you are trying to dissuade me from helping, but you are wrong that this is not my battle as well. Have you so easily forgotten I am the father of Lunadar's heir? Candra is destined to rule both the realms of Lunadar and Renndar one day, and as such I am honor bound to ensure Lunadar's current leader has every opportunity to complete a successful mission if such a thing is in the gods' plans. Besides, you promised me, should you ever did battle with Lord Shemar, you would not turn away my help."

Ariana thought over the prince's words and could find no fault in his view of the situation. For what seemed like the first time in forever, she allowed a smile to light up her face as she extended a hand to the prince. "When you put it so eloquently, how can I refuse such an offer? As Lunadar's leader I accept your kind offer and will do everything in my power to see your emissaries return safely to Renndar."

A twinkle returned to Prince Kaspar's eye as he grasped Ariana's outstretched hand in his own. Immediately she could feel the heat searing her fingers but before she could withdraw them, the merman leaned over and gently placed a kiss on the back of her hand. Laughing at the surprised look on her face, the prince smiled and said, "Like I've said before, Ariana, you have but to command me, and I would gladly do your bidding, no matter the cost."

And with those words, Prince Kaspar bowed low and dove into the waves, leaving Ariana to stare at the place where he was just a moment before. Shaking her head to clear her thoughts, Ariana returned to her chambers and climbed into bed.

She refused to acknowledge the butterflies still hovering around inside but instead, pulled the coverlet over her and promptly drifted off to sleep. There would be time enough later to analyze that kiss and this new development between herself and the prince, but for now she needed to prepare herself for the upcoming battle with rest.

173

CHAPTER TWENTY

Ariana had never ventured beyond Tumac Mountain to the wasteland Lord Shemar called home. The three days had passed quickly, and now two columns of armored men moved in tandem behind her. Aramid hadn't been ridden enough lately and was a bit spirited but nothing Ariana couldn't handle.

Beside her Alasdair rode quietly, continuously surveying the horizon in all directions as if he expected the Drundles to materialize out of thin air. Pulling her mount closer to the captain of her guards, Ariana lowered her voice and asked, "Do you see something out there which makes you look like you are expecting the devil himself to appear?"

Alasdair glanced quickly in Ariana's direction before continuing to survey their surroundings. "Lord Shemar is not far from being such a creature, milady. I would be remiss in my duties if I were to allow the dark lord or his Drundles to come upon us unaware."

"I meant no rebuff in my words, Alasdair. I was merely observing how diligently you are watching out for us. Are you apprehensive of what lies before us?"

"I would be foolish not to admit I would prefer to handle Lord Shemar in some other, less perilous, manner."

"As would I, Alasdair, but I see no other course available for us. Do you think the fact that any one of us may not be returning home at the end of this quest does not weigh heavily on my heart? I have heard enough of my people dying to last me a lifetime. Therefore, the dark lord must be stopped at any cost!"

Alasdair looked back at the men willingly following their leader into battle. Many of these same men had served King Midar and were aware of what the Drundles can do to a man. A few were even part of the last attempt to recover the Cup of Notari and watched their friends fall under the dark lord's counterattack. Still, they offered their lives in service to the realm and the belief Ariana would bring them into the light of a redeemed Lunadar. Alasdair turned back in his saddle to face Ariana once more.

"Milady, I believe this quest is a just one. Only the gods know the outcome, but there is one thing I do know. Future historians will look back on today and only see a fearless leader and the men who chose to follow her through the gates of hell if need be to secure the future of Lunadar."

Ariana glanced back at her men once more before saying, "I pray you are right, Alasdair. We all have but one life to give to a noble cause. While I do not choose to lose my life to Lord Shemar today, I am at peace with my decision to make this quest to return the Cup of Notari to its rightful owner."

Alasdair suddenly pulled up short, causing Ariana to stop as well, and pointed to the left toward a dark outcropping on the side of Tumac Mountain. They were still too far away to identify how many Drundles guarded Lord Shemar's castle, but even from this vantage point she could feel the evil surrounding the entrance as if some wild beast crouched nearby just waiting to strike. Sitting tall in the saddle, Ariana said, "I presume that is Lord Shemar's castle."

"That it is, milady."

"Very well. I will speak to the men and then you may give the command to move forward."

Ariana broke out of formation and rode past the columns to circle around the lines before making her way back to the head of the two regiments. Raising her hand to command the men's attention, Ariana stood tall in her saddle and said, "It is time, men, for each one of us to meet our destiny head on. Only the gods know which of us will be successful on this quest and which of us may spill our blood on the battlefield in honor of my father, King Midar. You honor me with your service, and I am proud to stand among you as we go into battle!"

As one, the men raised their swords in silent salute to their leader before beginning their trek up the mountainside on Alasdair's command. They met with no resistance until they were fifty yards from the castle's entrance. Suddenly to the right of them there came an unearthly sound as screeching Drundles broke from the shadows to come down the mountainside to meet them.

The ungodly sound of screaming Drundles startled Aramid and he reared back, almost unseating Ariana. Struggling momentarily to control the stallion, she saw Alasdair motion for his regiment to charge forward to meet Lord Shemar's minions head on. Shouting out in vain for Alasdair to stop before he met certain death, Ariana motioned for her men to follow him.

Poisonous barbs began to shower down on the first of Ariana's guards as they came within range of the Drundles' deadly aim. One by one her guards screamed in agony as the barbs reached their targets, and in a horrifying instant Ariana realized how futile this quest was.

The dark lord's castle could not be breached as long as he had his Drundles to protect him. Pulling hard on Aramid's reins, Ariana yelled for her guards to retreat. The line of Drundles had almost reached Alasdair, and she heard herself scream when the first barb struck him. His own screams of agony mingled with others around him. Ariana watched in horror as he slipped from his horse to fall dead in the path of oncoming Drundles.

As she watched Lord Shemar's minions bear down in her direction, Ariana knew she should retreat but shock rooted her to her spot. How foolish of her to think she could challenge the gods to allow her to follow her own path and not suffer the consequences of her arrogance. Now Alasdair had just paid the ultimate price for following her in some ridiculous quest. Ariana was so lost in thought it took the hissing sound of a Drundles barb whizzing by her head to shock her back to the present. Digging her heels into Aramid's side as she pulled hard on the reins, the stallion lunged into a gallop as she raced to catch up to her retreating guards.

Dust kicked up under Aramid's pounding hooves as the stallion tried to pull away from the charging Drundles. If she could just make it to Dreydan's Falls the water would protect her. Ariana crouched low over the stallion withers as more barbs whizzed past her. There was no time to process the fact Alasdair was left behind. No time to count the many lives she would have to atone for if she made it back to Lunadar alive.

Unchecked tears streamed down Ariana's face as she saw the first of her remaining guards reach the falls. If they could just make it to the other side they might have a chance to escape. The sound of the Drundles screeching in anger was beginning to fade which told her Aramid was outrunning them. Just as she looked over her shoulder to see how far behind the creatures were, she felt Aramid stumble and try in vain to stop itself from falling. She didn't even have time to react before she felt herself tumble out of the saddle and come to a jolting stop as she hit the banks of the river lying just beyond Dreydan's Falls.

Ariana lay dazed on the ground for a moment before struggling to her feet. The sound of the advancing Drundles was getting louder, and she had mere seconds before they would be upon her. Despite the sharp pain in her side whenever she took a breath, Ariana began to stumble toward the water. It was her only chance to make it out of this deadly situation. Fear spurred her on as the sounds of screeching filled her ears. Crying out to the gods for mercy, Ariana dove into the water at the base of the falls just as the Drundles came into range of letting lose their deadly barbs.

Ariana broke the surface to discover she was not alone. Dozens of water sprites surrounded her with bows drawn. She could hear the Drundles screams of pain and could smell the burning flesh as wave after wave of water-filled arrows hit their mark.

She could only watch in amazement as the Drundles fled in terror back in the direction of Lord Shemar's castle. Suddenly feeling lightheaded, Ariana managed to swim to the water's edge and crawl onto higher ground before a curtain of darkness descended upon her.

CHAPTER TWENTY-ONE

Ariana felt like she was drowning in quicksand while all around her the guards were cut down until there was nothing left but a sea of blood and bodies. Screaming out Alasdair's name, Ariana woke up in a sweat and realized it had all been a horrible nightmare. Except for the fact the captain of her guards was no longer alive because of her, and the families of those who perished would never be able to forgive her.

It had been three days since the terrible day outside Lord Shemar's castle, and Ariana still could not sleep without Alasdair's screams haunting her every time she closed her eyes to rest. The water sprites had watched over her until someone returned to carry her back to Lunadar, but who could save her from herself and the demons tormenting her now?

Oh, Father, what have I done in your name? What kind of leader would send men into battle against such odds? And who was I, a mere mystic, to challenge the gods like that? Ariana flung back the coverlet and threw on her wrap. If she remained within these castle walls she feared she would go mad. Deep down she knew there was only one person who could still the demons raging inside her head.

Only one creature who seemed to know her soul better than she knew herself.

Leaving the castle, Ariana made her way to the pools beneath her balcony. She didn't stop to question the madness of her actions but simply let her feet follow the sound of the mermaid's song leading her to the water. Removing her wrap and laying it on nearby stones, Ariana slipped quietly into the cool water and waited for the sea creature she knew would come to her from the deep.

Ariana's eyes had just begun to adjust to the darkness when she saw him rise from beneath the waves and glide to within a few feet in front of her. How could she have thought the color of his eyes were sea green? The eyes seeming to stare right through her now were slate grey like storm clouds before a summer's rain. Chill bumps raced up Ariana's arms at those same eyes seem to glow like molten steel as the prince quietly studied her face, and she shivered in the cool night air. Covering the distance between them, his silky voice seemed to caress her as the prince whispered, "Ariana, why did you answer the mermaid song's call? Why are you here?"

Suddenly Ariana felt nervous and retreated from the prince until her back felt the smooth stones at the edge of the pool. Shyly she looked away and replied, "In truth, I'm not sure. I awoke from a nightmare and sought comfort from the demons that follow me ever since I've returned from Lord Shemar's castle."

Prince Kaspar inched closer to Ariana once more, not wanting to break the song's spell, and said, "And you thought I could rid you of these demons?"

Ariana almost chose not to answer the prince's question but finally, in a small voice, said, "Yes." She peeked out at the prince from beneath her lashes and saw those same grey eyes change again to almost black as he closed the distance between them to gently grasp her shoulders.

Reaching out one hand to tilt Ariana's face into the moonlight, Prince Kaspar studied her for a moment before saying in a low, husky voice, "Do you realize, milady, that my prediction has come true? That you have finally stopped fighting the call of the mermaid's song and have come to me of your own free will?"

Trembling, Ariana attempted to break contact with Prince Kaspar, but he refused to release her. She knew he would have more questions and even now, sharing the moonlight with him, she wasn't sure what her answers would be.

"Ariana, what do you ask of me? I would think you would be well versed in the legends surrounding answering such a call. Coming to me is an act of betrothal in the eyes of the gods. I am at a loss as to why you would do such a thing when you have made yourself abundantly clear you have no wish to join your life to mine."

Ariana opened her lips to speak but no words came out. *How could she tell him of her despair over the death of her friend and confidant, Alasdair? How could he understand the unforgiving weight of responsibility on her shoulders as leader of Lunadar?* She could only look at him as tears began to stream down her face.

Pulling her into his arms, Prince Kaspar held her tightly against his chest and whispered words of comfort as the storm broke over Ariana's soul. Time seemed to slow down as merman and mystic clung to each other in the moonlight. Slowly the storm passed, and Ariana's tears slowed as she pushed against the prince's chest to break the contact between them. Reluctantly releasing her, Prince Kaspar kept one arm captive as Ariana struggled to regain her composure. He caressed the inside of one wrist with a sea-roughened thumb, and Ariana could feel her pulse quicken at his touch.

Once again, the prince attempted to break through the wall Ariana had built around her heart. "Ariana, do you not realize by now that you are as vital to me as breath itself, and I cannot bear to see you in such pain? Come, share your burden with me, milady, and allow me to lighten your load."

Taking a deep breath, Ariana turned her back on those fears lurking in the shadows of her mind and gazed into the dark waters below her. In a low voice full of unshed tears, Ariana replied, "I knew what I was doing when I answered the mermaid's song.

My heart is weary from all this fighting between us. My body is weary of fighting battles I can never seem to win. My very soul is weary of this yoke of responsibility I never asked for when my father was killed in battle. When I awoke tonight from yet another nightmare to feel the anguish once again at being responsible for Alasdair's death, I wanted to simply run away from my beloved Lunadar."

Prince Kaspar reached out to cup Ariana's chin in his hand and gently forced her to look at him. "You cannot count yourself responsible for Alasdair's death, my love. His way was a warrior's way, and his was an honorable death."

"But it is my fault! If it had not been for that foolish quest to return the Cup of Notari to Quallan Forest, Alasdair would still be alive!"

The prince gently shook Ariana and said, "So you think you are one of the gods now? For only they know the course of a man's life. Alasdair's days were numbered, as are all of ours, so who's to say he wouldn't have fallen victim to a Drundle's barb the very next time he went beyond Lunadar's walls? The only thing we can all do is attempt to live our lives honorably, cherish our loved ones while we can, and hope the good we have done during our time in this realm won't be forgotten once we are gone."

Ariana stopped for a moment to think about the prince's words. While her heart still bled for the loss of her friend, she could not deny the wisdom in Prince Kaspar's words. Somehow Ariana knew when she came to the pools tonight that she would find answers to her prayers for peace. She just didn't realize it would come in the form of a former sea devil who managed to somehow capture her heart in the process of comforting her.

Staring at him through misty eyes, Ariana replied, "My prince, of course you are right. I will continue to deeply mourn the passing of my dear friend, Alasdair, but he was a warrior as you say and deserves a warrior's tribute not some wench weeping over his ashes."

Prince Kaspar cocked his head to one side and stared at Ariana for a moment before saying, "Why Ariana, did I just hear you say, 'my prince'? For, in truth, I could never belong to anyone else but you, milady."

Ariana could feel the blush creeping into her cheeks but for once she did not care if the prince saw it. Looking up at him with a shy smile, she replied, "It is entirely possible I may have called you that, Prince Kaspar, but you will have to prove yourself worthy before I might call you that again."

Ariana's breath caught in her throat when she saw the prince's eyes change once again to the sea green she knew so well. Those eyes seem to glow like jewels as he slowly pulled her back into his embrace and said, "Then, milady, let me but prove just how worthy these lips are to call you mine!"

Her senses suddenly seem to swirl all around her as the prince's lips lowered to meet hers. The kiss they had shared before was nothing to compare to this. Ariana felt like she was being branded for life, tied heart and soul to this merman who could crush her with his bare hands, but instead was caressing her with such intimacy she felt faint.

Too soon for her liking the prince lifted his lips from hers and smiled into the dazed eyes staring back at him. "I presume, milady, that I have proven myself of some worth to you?"

Ariana could only sigh, "Oh yes!"

Prince Kaspar chuckled before brushing a quick kiss on Ariana's lips once more before turning her toward the castle. "I think it is time for you to return to your chambers before I take any more advantage of this moonlight and mermaid's song."

"But…"

"No buts, Ariana. There will be plenty of time later to pursue such pleasures, but for now you need your rest, and I need my distance from those enticing lips. You can only expect me to be so strong but even a merman has his limits!" And with that, Prince Kaspar bowed low and dove into the waves to disappear. Ariana absently brushed her fingers against her lips and sighed. She had failed miserably in her fight against the call of the mermaid's song but right at this moment, somehow she didn't care.

CHAPTER TWENTY-TWO

The next few days were the most peaceful Ariana had felt in a long time. Despite the heavy heart she felt over the loss of Alasdair, Ariana managed to focus on counseling the people of Lunadar in daily matters as necessary and attend to her other obligations. At last, there was time to spend a few precious hours with her daughter. Time to heal a bruised spirit while cuddling with a child whose skin was soft as rose petals and whose hair smelled of sweet lavender.

At night, she would return to the pools and share a moonlit swim with her prince. Funny how an idea like conversing with Prince Kaspar, once repugnant to her, was the very thing her heart searched for these days. Playing with the otter family amongst the kelp beds reminded Ariana what it felt like to be young and carefree. They were so like the ones she spent time watching back at Shanty's Cove. Before her father was murdered. Before others depended on her leadership and guidance for their very survival. Before Winter's Solstice and her beloved daughter Candra.

Ariana looked around the great hall once more and shrugged her shoulders to help ease the tension gathering there. Today had been exceptionally long with an endless line of petitioners' squabbles to address and she was tired. Ariana was just about to motion for a break when the caller at the door herald a troop of visitors she did not expect to see back in Lunadar so soon after their last meeting.

Tomari seemed to float across the floor in her forest-colored gown in advance of her guards, until she halted before the throne where Ariana sat watching her entrance with much curiosity. Nodding regally to her, Ariana was the first to speak.

"Welcome, milady, to Lunadar. I am pleased you honor us with your presence. How may I be of service to you?"

Ignoring the villagers who openly stared at the visitor from Quallan Forest, Tomari offered a small curtsy in return before saying, "Greetings, Princess Ariana, daughter of King Midar. I have come bearing a personal invitation, on behalf of Queen Elysie, to attend a grand ball to be held at the queen's palace in two days' time."

Ariana concealed her surprise at Tomari's announcement. The last thing she presumed Queen Elysie wanted was to come face to face with her any time soon, and yet, here she extended her personal invitation to a ball. If her departure for the Otherworld wasn't a necessary evil she might have contemplated attending, but there was much to do, and her ship must be ready in less than a week's time.

"Please extend my sincerest apologies to Queen Elysie, but unfortunately there are pressing matters needing my attention here at Lunadar."

Tomari stepped closer to Ariana and replied, "I believe you misunderstand me, Princess Ariana. This ball is not merely a celebration of the seasons. Queen Elysie and the whole of Quallan Forest wish to create a ball to honor you."

Ariana was stunned. She could only stare at the woman standing before her. "Me? But why in the name of the gods would the queen want to do that?"

"To honor the Cup of Notari's hero, of course."

"Honor me? But I didn't complete my quest to return the cup to Quallan Forest. In fact, it was my foolishness which caused many of my men to lose their lives to the Drundles' barbs, including my captain of the guards. No, milady, I am the last person anyone should be honoring with a grand ball."

Tomari closed the distance between them to place her hand on Ariana's. "But that is where you are wrong, Princess Ariana. Yes, the quest you ventured out on was nearly impossible to achieve, but you did not let that stop you from leading your men to Lord Shemar's castle anyway. There is no shame to fail at such a task. The shame would have been to allow fear to prevent you from even trying. You are truly a hero in the eyes of the people of Quallan Forest. King Midar would have been proud to see you on the battlefield, even if it meant saving your men by retreating. Please allow the people of Quallan Forest to honor you for championing us in such a way."

Ariana was speechless. *Me? A hero? How can Queen Elysie and her people think of me as one? If they only knew the cowardess lurking inside this body. I should have been the one to lead the charge on Lord Shemar and his Drundles. I should have been the one to die in my saddle while Alasdair had the chance to live!*

Ariana gazed around the room to see the villagers holding their breath as they waited for her reply. These people who have believed in her since the day she ascended the throne. How could she take away their right to think her a hero as well if the people of Quallan Forest should already think it so?

Praying to the gods she was making the right decision, Ariana placed her hand on top of Tomari's and in a low voice replied, "Please tell your queen I would be deeply honored to attend such a ball. I can only hope I might continue to serve the interests of the people of Quallan Forest to the best of my ability for many years to come."

Tomari stepped away from the throne and dropped into a deep curtsy before Ariana. Rising once again, Tomari smiled. "The queen will be very pleased to hear you have kindly accepted our invitation. May the next two days be filled with peace and love until we meet again." After another graceful nod in Ariana's direction,

Tomari left the great hall among the excited whispers of the villagers as they discussed what had just transpired.

Ariana stood and motioned for her guards to lead the people from the room. There would be no more petitions read today. Her mind and body were weary. She would rest in her chambers until she could go to her prince once again.

Ariana lay down but could not rest. Something elusive seemed to keep nagging at the back of her mind. Alasdair's death and the failed quest kept bringing her back to memories of her father and that made her think of his mystery woman. Who in the world could she be? Realizing she would never have peace until she figured it out, Ariana lit her bedside candle and reached for the stack of papers lying nearby. Wondering what else her father had kept hidden from her, Ariana read another entry from her father's journal.

Night of the Moon Shadow

I know not why the gods have cursed me with a love for two women. One is the mother of my beautiful child and has earned the privilege to sit next to me on the throne. The other is a queen in her own right, a wise and mighty leader of her own realm, who only seeks to keep evil at bay. Why should I not champion her cause and attempt to return the thing most precious to her? She knows not yet of her man's betrayal and there may still be time to return the relic to its rightful place before any harm is done by this treachery.

Ariana dropped her father's papers from shock as she finally realized the object of his affection. Queen Elysie was the mysterious woman who had captured her father's heart, but when? How? Was it a love returned, or a lover scorned? The thoughts and unanswered questions swirling about the room drove Ariana to throw on her wrap and seek the refuge of the pools. Maybe the prince was already waiting there for her, and she could finally share this burden of doubt laying heavily on her spirit.

She had almost reached the smooth stones circling the pools when she heard the low humming notes of the mermaid's song. Quickening her step, she stopped at the water's edge to gaze at the merman lying on the rocks as he studied the stars twinkling above him.

For just a moment Prince Kaspar didn't know she watched him, and Ariana had a chance to drink her fill of his beauty. The love she was beginning to feel for him almost hurt for how would the gods ever let them be together?

Oh, my prince, in what realm would we live? In Lunadar where he would not stride through the countryside as a normal man could? Or in Renndar where I would be forced to live off underwater potions just to survive? And what about our child? Would she be forever destined to be torn between two worlds?

Prince Kaspar turned his head in time to see the worry settle deep in Ariana's eyes and called out to her, "Ariana, why do you worry so? What has caused the smile to leave your eyes?"

Walking slowly over to where he was, Ariana reached out to take his hand as he pulled her up to sit beside him. Silently he waited for her to come to him with whatever burden lay on her heart, causing the wave of sadness pulsating between them. Ariana attempted to put off the debate she knew would come once she told him of her worries and instead shared the news of the day.

"Tomari visited Lunadar today."

The prince looked at her in surprise. "Well, well, that is not exactly news I expected to hear from you today. May I ask what was the reason for her visit?"

Ariana studied the strong fingers holding hers a moment before replying, "She invited me to a ball at Quallan Forest in two days' time."

"An invitation to a ball brought her to you? I still don't understand."

Ariana gave a small sigh before continuing. "Queen Elysie wishes to honor me for my quest to return the Cup of Notari to Quallan Forest. I tried to dissuade Tomari and explained I am not the hero they think me to be, but she insisted I earned my rightful place in their honorarium room."

Prince Kaspar sat up straighter to stare at Ariana's bent head and said, "And you don't think you deserve such an honor?"

Ariana's head jerked up and she passionately replied, "How could you think I do? No matter your logic as to the outcome of my failed quest, the fact will always remain that I am the reason so many of my men are dead, and their children will reach out through their nightmares for fathers who will never again be able to kiss their tears away!"

The prince pulled Ariana into his arms to lean against him before saying, "So what was your answer to the queen's invitation?"

Ariana closed her eyes and leaned against his strong shoulder. "I had to bow to my people's wishes and accept Tomari's invitation. With all they have been through, how could I destroy their dream that their disappointing leader has somehow transformed into a mighty hero before their very eyes? If I had but known then what I know now about Queen Elysie, my answer might have been very different."

Prince Kaspar gently set Ariana aside to lift her chin up, forcing her to look at him. "And exactly what do you know now that would change the path you chose?"

At first, she wasn't sure how to answer such a question. *Share your burdens with me* the prince had once told her and now was the time to test his words. Pulling her chin from his strong fingers, Ariana lifted it even higher and said, "I read more of my father's journal before I came to you. I have discovered the mystery woman my father yearned for was none other than Queen Elysie herself!"

"Queen Elysie? But how can that be? Are you sure?"

"Oh yes, my father made it quite clear he sought to be her champion and started that foolish quest to recover the relic, and I presume demonstrate the depth of his love for her by returning it to its rightful home."

"But what of your mother? Was she aware of the king's affections for another? Was that love even consummated?"

The very questions Ariana asked herself, and she was still no closer to answers than she was earlier that evening. Instead of answering the prince, Ariana slid from the rocks to remove her wrap and dive into the cooling waters. Agitated, she moved about restlessly while Prince Kaspar swam easily by her side. It was some time later when Ariana finally slowed down to catch her breath, and the prince reached out to tuck tendrils of hair behind her ears.

The shadows of the night could not hide the worry still lurking in her eyes, prompting Prince Kaspar to say, "Ariana, what troubles you so? In truth, I do not believe the worry I see in your eyes to be caused by a possible affair between your father and the queen of Quallan Forest. I know you. Something else troubles your heart, and I wish you would let me share your burdens, whatever they might be."

There it was again. *Share your burdens with me.* Knowing he would not like what she was about to say, Ariana plunged ahead anyway.

"Kaspar, you know you are my prince and the father of my child, but no matter how I try to come to terms with it, we are from different realms. I am the rightful leader of Lunadar while you are the future heir of Renndar. We are like the Unicorn and the Kelpie. They might both love each other, but where would they build their home?"

Ariana saw the prince's eyes begin to turn a dark shade of grey and she knew she had angered him with her question.

"So, should I be led to believe you doubt us having a chance to make things work between us?"

"You must agree, my love, that we both have different opinions about Candra's future. I have already begun her training to take her rightful place on the throne of Lunadar one day. My daughter knows no other life."

Prince Kaspar moved away from Ariana to cross his arms and say, "Don't you mean to say our daughter? For it was not my fault I was not able to be a father to her all these years. I lay that blame at your door, Ariana. You knew I would not forsake my own blood, and yet you continued to deceive me at every turn."

Ariana could feel her own anger rise unchecked as she stared back at him. "And how was I to know that I might be allowed to ask? For all I knew of you then was that you were a sea devil hiding behind the spell of a mermaid's song, so you could seduce young maids during a winter's celebration. That was not the father I wished for Candra!"

The prince stared speechless at her for a moment. Ariana was not sure if she had gone too far; if the merman's anger would explode to wash over her so she was surprised when he finally spoke.

"And now, Ariana? What kind of man and father do you think of me now? Do you really know so little of me to think I would ever do anything to harm either you or our child? Do you not realize I would willingly give my life for you if it were to ever come to that?

I endangered my own chances of a rightful inheritance to the realm of Renndar when I pulled you from my mother's reach, and still, you doubt the depths of my feelings for you. What will it take, Ariana, for you to believe? You may be right, milady. The gods may be against us after all."

Without allowing Ariana to reply, the prince took one more look at her before turning his back on her and slipping under the waters. Ariana called out to him, but all she heard was the sound of waterfalls in the distance. Even the soft, undulating sound of the mermaid's song had left her.

Wiping away tears suddenly stinging her eyes, Ariana retrieved her wrap and with a heavy heart returned to her bedchamber. *What have I done? I should be looking to a future with Prince Kaspar, and instead I fear I have driven him away forever!* Ariana managed to make it to her bed before the tears began to fall, and it was much later before she finally cried herself to sleep.

CHAPTER TWENTY-THREE

It was as if a million stars had been pulled down from the heavens to light up Quallan Forest as Ariana quietly stepped on the path leading into the heart of the woods. It had been a rough two days. There was no sight of the prince, and her men were readying the ship for yet another pirate's run to the Otherworld.

Her mind was kept busy during daylight hours with the everyday affairs of running Lunadar, but her body found no peace at night when the moonlight beckoned to her from the pools. What once was dreaded, Ariana now looked forward to the ball if only to distract her from running that last night with Prince Kaspar again in her mind.

Tomorrow, she sailed for the portal. She could only pray to the gods she would find a way to reach out to the prince once she returned. She had so much to atone for. So much over which to ask his forgiveness. She had been so foolish for so long, and now there was a real chance she had indeed discovered a way to break the spell of the mermaid's song. Only now, if she were honest with herself, would she gladly in an instant hand over her heart to that merman for safekeeping.

Ariana almost stumbled over the edge of her gown when Tomari suddenly appeared before her. Leaves of orange, burnt sienna, and jade had been woven together into a stunning gown which put the trees around them to shame. Raindrops had been captured to adorn the silver necklace on her neck and dripping from her ears.

Ariana could only hope her own gown would meet with the queen's approval as she brushed her fingers nervously against the silver silk trimmed in black. Her lady's maid had swept her hair to one side and tiny white pearls peeked throughout her ebony tresses. Nodding to her host, Ariana called out a greeting.

"Milady, how stunning you look. You must be the fairest of the fair in all Quallan Forest."

"Why, Princess Ariana, you must realize there is no one under the moon who can outshine your own loveliness. We of this realm are honored by your presence. Come, let us set aside these formalities and make our way to the ball. It is a night of great celebration, and the queen is so pleased to know you have arrived."

As the two women made their way toward the castle, Ariana could hear the fairies of Quallan Forest whispering all around her, murmuring things like 'hero', 'brave one', and 'Gwenllian'. She turned to Tomari to ask, "Why do the fairies call out 'Gwenllian'?"

"That is the name of one of our history's greatest women warriors. Gwenllian once led an army against outsiders seeking to invade our realm. Her own quest was met with defeat, not unlike your own, but she showed such strength against all odds that our people paid tribute to her bravery and wish to honor you in the same way."

Ariana was humbled by the knowledge these people believed her to be like that other woman. She felt like she was somehow being dishonest to Gwenllian's memory by accepting such an invitation, but there was no turning back now as they had arrived at Queen Elysie's castle. She could only move forward with this tribute and pray to the gods one day she would be worthy of the honor being bestowed on her this night.

Hours later, Ariana could no longer sit ramrod straight against the inviting cushions tempting her from behind. The receiving room had been magically changed into a hall of wonder with glittering chandeliers made from stag horns and large silk cushions thrown all about the floor. She had been sitting for what seemed forever as dancers in flowing ethereal gowns performed to the music pulsating all around her.

Ariana should have known better than to presume this ball would be a formal affair with strict rules of conduct. This was, after all, a fairies' ball and the stuff of which legends were made.

Finally allowing herself to relax against a cushion for a moment, Ariana studied the musicians playing in one corner of the vast room. The surreal tones of the Ocarina wove its way around the frenzied sound of the Tanbur while the plucked chimes ringing out from the metal bars of the Mbira dueled with the low, eerie, harmonic drone of the Didgeridoo. Music speaking to one's soul and bewitching anyone near enough to hear.

Suddenly feeling like she couldn't breathe, Ariana quickly stood up and made her way to an alcove just outside the grand hall. Stopping to catch her breath, Ariana didn't notice she wasn't alone until she heard the faint giggling of a young child.

Looking around the small room, at first, she saw no one until bright hazel eyes peeked out from behind a tapestry curtain. A male Fairie, just a few years older than Candra, looked at Ariana with wide eyed wonder and was about to dash from the room when Ariana dropped to her knees in front of him.

"Please do not be afraid", she said. "I have only come to rest a bit and didn't mean to startle you."

The child must have decided to trust her as he moved away from the curtain and stepped into the room. Tilting his head to one side, the young boy finally gave Ariana a wide, toothy grin and said, "You must be the Brave One my father tells me about."

"And who is your father?"

The boy stood taller and thrusting his Fairie wings behind him, he replied, "Why, I am the son of Alewar, captain of Queen Elysie's unicorn guards!"

Ariana hid a smile as she heard the pride in the young boy's voice.

"I am honored to meet such a fine young Fairie such as yourself. I am the Princess Ariana, but I must confess I am at a loss as I do not know your name."

The young Fairie bowed so low his sandy colored hair almost touched his boots before rising to look at Ariana once again.

"My name is Aningan."

Ariana smiled at the Fairie before rising to her feet and saying, "A strong name indeed for such a small boy but no matter. You will have many years in which to grow into a name such as that one. Why are you hiding in here I wonder?"

Aningan broke into another wide grin and replied, "My guardian told me it was my bedtime, but I just couldn't sleep without seeing at least some of the ball, so I ran away when she was preparing my bath!"

Just as my sweet Candra would have done. I think these two could be great friends one day if it is in the gods' plans. Ariana gently placed her hand on the top of Aningan's head and said, "I agree that one should be allowed to glimpse the magic of such a fine Fairie ball, but do you not think it is time you return to your bed chambers? I am sure your guardian will be frantic with worry. I know I would be if my own Candra were missing."

"You have a child?"

"Yes, my daughter is just a wee bit younger than you, but I think you two could become friends one day."

Aningan placed his fists on his tunic's sash and shook his head. "Oh no, Princess Ariana, that could never be."

"But why ever not, Aningan?

The young Fairie scrunched up his nose and replied, "Why, because girls are so yucky!"

Ariana burst out laughing as Aningan quickly bowed once again before dashing out of the room. The encounter with the young Fairie was just what she needed to lighten her spirits.

All she wanted to do was return to Lunadar, but the honoring ceremony was about to begin, and she was duty bound to remain until it was over. Giving a little sigh before straightening her shoulders, Ariana moved to return to the festivities when she almost bumped into the queen's daughter as she entered the alcove.

Ariana could see there were many questions lurking in Tomari's eyes as the Fairie glanced quickly about the room, but she simply said, "Is all well with you, Princess Ariana? The queen noticed your departure from the celebration and wondered if our ball was somehow not to your liking?"

"No, that is not it at all, milady. I was momentarily overwhelmed by the beauty of your people's wonderful dancing and but sought a quiet moment to compose myself. In fact, I was about to return to the ball when you came in search of me."

Tomari said nothing more but stepped aside to allow Ariana to accompany her back to the receiving room. She noticed the music had stopped, and all eyes were watching her return. Tomari motioned for her to advance to the throne, and Ariana realized this was the moment she had been dreading all evening.

Dear gods, I am not worthy of this honor the people of Quallan Forest are trying to bestow on me. My father was their champion, not I. Nor am I like this Gwenllian of whom they speak. My own so-called bravery was born of fear, not strength. These people would shun me if they knew of my deceit, but how can I destroy their reason to believe in their dreams of what could have been? Even my own people think me a hero and their spirits are renewed by this honorarium. How can I speak the truth of my foolish actions now and destroy my own people's faith in their leader?

Ariana realized Tomari had left her side to stand next to the queen. She finally reached the edge of the dais where Queen Elysie stood watching her approach. Making a sweeping gesture with one arm, the queen called out to the room, "People of this realm, we have before us the daughter of the mighty King Midar, champion to Quallan Forest and the Cup of Notari. Once that magical relic lay safe within these castle walls before Lord Shemar sought to make it his own. King

Midar sacrificed his own life in the service of this realm, and we will forever honor his name.

Now let it be known to the four corners of Quallan Forest that we have found yet another champion of our realm in the brave Princess Ariana!"

Thunderous applause and cheering met with the queen's words while Ariana merely bowed her head in silence. Queen Elysie continued, "A quest which ends in defeat may still be a journey worth taking. Lunadar's leader knew the odds of overcoming the Drundles on the battlefield and yet she still faced the challenge set before her. Like the great Gwenllian, our children's children will speak of Princess Ariana with honor and thankfulness for all she attempted to do in the name of the people of Quallan Forrest.

Again, thunderous applause and cheering erupted throughout the hall as Queen Elysie motioned for Ariana to step forward before taking two silver medallions from Tomari. Raising them skyward, the queen repeated the ancient prayer of offering to the gods before motioning for Ariana to kneel before her.

"Princess Ariana, the bonds between a leader and her people are strong. The bonds of a mother and her child are even stronger. For championing my people and risking your own life in service to this realm, all of Quallan Forest honor you with this token of our gratitude for your bravery on the battlefield."

Queen Elysie placed the medallions around Ariana's neck before continuing. "No matter where you are, in this realm or the Otherworld, these relics will allow you to forever watch over those you love. A mere wave over water and the calling of their name will bring their image to you. Should your daughter ever have need of her mother, a wave of her hand and a whisper of your name will bring your image to her. In this manner, the bond you two share shall remain forged forever."

More cheers filled the room as Ariana held the medallions in her hand. At first, they were cool to touch but soon warmth seemed to radiate from the relics and Ariana's eyes moistened at the thought of her daughter. *Forever linked to my sweet Candra, no matter where the seas may take me. How did Queen Elysie know this is what my heart had been looking for all along?*

Ariana looked at the queen through misty eyes and said in a low voice, "This precious gift is more than I deserve. I am deeply touched by what the people of Quallan Forest have done to honor the memory of my father, King Midar. I can only pray to the gods that our two realms might continue to be joined in a mutual brotherhood for many millenniums to come. Thank you for this honor."

Music began to fill the room once more as the formalities were completed and the celebration continued well on into the night. Ariana kept up appearances for a short time more before begging leave to prepare for her ship's departure the following day. Everyone wished her to remain, but duty was a harsh taskmaster, and the portal would wait for no one.

CHAPTER TWENTY-FOUR

Ariana lowered the eyeglass and sighed again. Nothing broke the surface of the calm waters surrounding her. Her fingers played with the medallions hanging around her neck as she absently gave orders to her men. She should have been happy there were no warships on the horizon, but instead she only felt a restlessness building deep inside her.

The portal was due to open at any moment and her time in the Otherworld would be over once again. This pirating life was becoming almost too easy, and it weighed heavily on Ariana's mind. The luck of the gods had been on her side but for how long? And at what price?

Ariana studied the medallions in her hand more closely. There had been no time once she returned to Lunadar from Quallan Forest to give Candra her relic. No time to explain to her young daughter the precious gift the queen had given them. Maybe the fact she was unable to spend time with her daughter before they sailed was causing this restlessness she felt?

Ariana looked at the moon, laying low in the water, and her mind could almost convince herself this was the case, but her heart knew differently. *How long had it been?*

How long since your body swayed in time to the mermaid's song? How long since you have seen those stormy eyes looking back into your own?

Ariana glanced around the ship's deck and a part of her was glad to see the rest of the men had retired to their chambers. While she would have welcomed a chance to run away from such thoughts again, deep down Ariana knew it was time she faced them head on. Gripping the ship's wheel tighter, Ariana allowed herself to think back to the last conversation she'd had with Prince Kaspar.

How well she remembers her foolish anger at his suggestion their futures become entwined. What seemed like sheer madness back then had somehow become a tantalizing daydream of late which refused to leave her no matter how much Ariana attempted to turn her thoughts elsewhere.

Even now, all she need do is close her eyes for the image of the merman's strong countenance to appear before her. All she need do is touch tongue to lips to taste again the saltiness of his kiss. Ariana rested her head against the rough grain of the wood beneath her hands and allowed a lone tear to escape.

She could no longer fight her feelings for Prince Kaspar, and now there may never be a chance to tell him of her love. It had been weeks since she heard the haunting melody of the mermaid's song to announce his presence, and Ariana feared she would never hear such a sweet sound again.

Were the gods really against them after all?

Ariana was so lost in her thoughts she did not hear the low sound when it began skimming across the waves toward her. Soft at first, the song grew louder as the familiar melody curled around her to caress her soul and her body began to sway to the almost forgotten melody. Ariana was almost afraid to open her eyes in case it was another dream.

Lifting her head, Ariana slowly walked to the bow of the ship and looked down into the deep green eyes of her prince. For a moment merman and mystic could only drink in the sight of each other. A soft sigh escaped Ariana's lips as she said in a voice full of tears, "I thought I would never see you again!"

"Oh, my sweet love, how could I stay away?"

"But the mermaid's song. When I could no longer hear it, I thought the spell had been broken forever."

Waves pushed against the ship as Prince Kaspar rose higher in the water to caress Ariana with his eyes before replying in a voice roughened by deep emotion, "The spell of the mermaid's song can never be broken unless the merman wishes it so. I told you before, Ariana, my heart belongs to you. You are my life and the air I breathe, and it will continue to be so until the day we are no more."

Tears began to slide down Ariana's cheeks as she bowed her head and said in a small voice, "You said the gods might be against us. You abandoned the 'us' we had created. I was beginning to believe and then you took your song with you. How was I to know if you would ever return to me?"

The prince slid through the water to reach the side of the ship. Balancing on the tip of his tail, Kaspar lifted himself high above the waves and reached out to grasp Ariana's cold hands in his. Almost instantly Ariana could feel the heat radiating from his body and curl up her arms to make her heart skip a beat before beginning to pound in a rhythm to match his.

Gently pulling Ariana closer to him, the prince lifted her chin to capture the fear he saw lurking in her eyes before saying in a silky voice Ariana knew so well, "Oh, my love, what a fool I have been these past few weeks to not return to your side. I had hoped putting distance between us would help you realize we are, in truth, of one spirit.

"Ariana, you know I come from a proud heritage of sea people. It is no different from the mighty lineage you come from when you stand in the light of Lunadar to defend its legacy. But don't you see? Two mighty realms have already joined together in our daughter, Candra. The gods have already blessed our union on that Winter Solstice's night so long ago. There is no need for this fear of love between us. It has already been written in the stars. All we need to do now is but listen to the mermaid's song and allow it to guide us to our hearts' desires."

Prince Kaspar drew Ariana closer to him until at last their lips met. Deep in her heart she knew what her prince said was true. The touch of his lips on hers was like finally coming home. Prince Kaspar was offering her his life and his love to her. She need only give hers in return to complete the song already swirling around them. Ariana gave herself up to his kiss.

The crashing sound of a cannonball splintering part of the deck behind Ariana startled the two of them apart, both turning to see a dark ship crouching low in the water between them and the now opened portal. At first Ariana could not make out what colors the ship flew. As another volley of cannonballs struck the ship, her heart leaped into her throat as she recognized the devil's flame and crossbones waving in the breeze.

Lord Shemar had caught them unawares and now stood between the ship and their way home. Turning to the prince, Ariana shouted to him, "I beg you flee this area. If I cannot beat Lord Shemar in battle, I will be forced to conjure up the winds to remove him from my path and you might be injured in the process!"

Prince Kaspar had to shout to be heard above the shouting of the men now running across the deck to man their battle stations. "I will not leave you! I will not let that devil tear the mother of my child from me!"

Ariana ran to grasp the wheel and pulled with all her might. If she could turn the ship broadside, it might be possible to release their own cannon fire and strike down the dark lord where he stood. Shouting orders to her men to come about, she could only pray as her men strained at the oars. There was another deafening boom before, as if in slow motion, Ariana could hear the snapping of the main mast as it crashed onto the deck below.

All that could be heard was the screams of the wounded as she fought to control the bucking ship underneath her. Without her sails, the ship could not survive a run to the portal. Lord Shemar had planned well his surprise and the only thing left for Ariana was to call upon her mystic powers in the hope it would be enough to ensure her men's safe return home.

Not looking around to see if Prince Kaspar heeded her warning to leave, Ariana could see the devil's flame and crossbones barreling down on her starboard side towards them as her hand briefly brushed against the medallions she wore. Glancing down at them, Ariana thought to herself, *Oh, Candra, my dearest one. I fear I have failed to do my duty to Lunadar and to you. There was no time to share Queen Elysie's gift with you, and now only the gods know if I will ever see your beautiful face again. May you always remember how much your mother loved you.*

Crying out to the gods as another cannon ball struck in front of her, Ariana struggled to calm her spirit and invoke the power of the winds. The image of her father, King Midar, came to her and her hair began to float above her as she chanted the ancient words. Ariana focused on his face. *I may never get the chance to read the rest of your journal, my father. I hope you have been proud of the leader I have sought to be in your absence. I pray the gods have mercy on my men should this be how my journey ends.*

The winds began to howl as Ariana beckoned for them to come to her aid. She almost didn't hear it at first, but suddenly the screams of a child could be heard floating across the waves to her. Stopping the ancient chant for a moment, Ariana listened again and thought her own heart had stopped beating when she recognized the voice of her own daughter screaming for her to silence the winds.

Breaking the spell, Ariana opened her eyes and ran to the railing as confusion turned to horror at the sight in front of her. Lord Shemar's ship had managed to come alongside her own. Moonlight streamed across the waters to illuminated Macklebee standing on the bridge next to the dark lord, the manservant's head hanging low in shame.

What is Macklebee doing with Lord Shemar? Ariana wondered. Confusion quickly turned to horror as Ariana noticed Candra being held captive in the arms of the dark lord.

Clutching the deck's railing, Ariana's angry voice easily carried across the waves.

"Macklebee, why have you done this terrible deed? Does your sense of loyalty mean nothing to you that you would endanger the life of an innocent?"

Her manservant only hung his head lower as a deep, rumbling laugh carried back on the wind to Ariana.

"And, Lord Shemar, if one hair on my daughter's head comes to any harm, I will hunt you to the depths of Abaddon to make you pay for what you have done!"

The dark lord just replied with another laugh, sending chills racing down Ariana's spine. He only tightened his grip on Candra and looked down his nose in contempt at Ariana.

"Well, well, Lady Ariana. We finally meet face to face on the battlefield. My Drundles have failed all this time to make you pay for your father's transgressions, but by the gods, today I will have my revenge!"

Ariana shook her head at his words. "What transgressions? What price did my father have to pay simply for loving another? The choice was my mother's to make, and she chose a king over the likes of you!"

Lord Shemar tightened his grip on the child by his side and Candra cried out in pain. "It would do well, milady, for you to remember in whose presence you now are in. Soon the portal will close and the future of Lunadar will be no more."

Ariana looked at the moon and realized the dark lord was correct. The moon dipped even lower in the water and the portal's light had begun to slowly dim. Looking around the deck, she could see the horror reflected in the eyes of her men as their way home was about to disappear from them forever. A voice she knew well and loved called out to Lord Shemar from the waves.

"You may have crippled Princess Ariana's ship, but I promise you, Lord Shemar, I will finish what has begun here should any harm come to that child."

The dark lord turned to look at the merman rising in the water to his full height before him. One glance between the two of them and Lord Shemar suddenly laughed out loud. "So, this is the way of things, is it? I was beginning to say the heir to Renndar has no place interfering with what is between Lady Ariana and myself, but I see I am mistaken.

You may be this child's father, Prince Kaspar, but even you will not be able to save them both, so which will you choose to champion? The mother of your child and leader of Lunadar? Or the future heir to Renndar? For I promise you, merman, you will not be able to save both!"

Lord Shemar turned his attention back to Ariana. "And which would you choose, milady, if given the chance to offer freedom to someone? Who are you willing to sacrifice in exchange for the life of your daughter or even the lives of your men?"

Ariana looked at Prince Kaspar and knew in her heart he was barely able to contain his fury. It was only a matter of seconds before her prince would do something foolish to protect those he loved, and she could not allow him to sacrifice his own life for her moment of foolishness. Turning back to Lord Shemar, Ariana called out to the dark lord, "What sacrifice do you speak of?"

She knew Lord Shemar realized how close the prince was to moving against him when the dark lord slowly smiled and replied with an almost conversational tone, "Why, it's quite simple really." Reaching into a pouch hanging low by his side, Lord Shemar removed a goblet and held it high above his head. Ariana could only look at it in shock as she realized what the dark lord held in his hand.

The Cup of Notari.

Even as the moon continued to dip ever lower into the sea, its light reflected off the many jewels encrusted on the goblet's surface until it seemed to shimmer in Lord Shemar's hand. "You get to decide the fate of everyone here, Lady Ariana. As I'm sure you know, one can only summon the power of the Cup of Notari at a great price.

I have traveled to the Otherworld outside of the portal to extract my revenge. Your men are of no consequence to me and my fight is not with them. I will even guarantee them safe passage onboard my ship back to Lunadar should they decide to accept my offer.

You, however, will not be so lucky for you must decide who will remain forever in the Otherworld, you or your daughter!"

"But what you ask of me is madness! I could never banish my own flesh and blood to live their lives in exile from all they have known!"

In a voice full of venom, Lord Shemar replied, "And yet, that is the very fate I am told you planned for me!"

Prince Kaspar did not hesitate but instantly shouted, "Take me, Lord Shemar! I freely offer my life in exchange for theirs!"

Lord Shemar didn't even glance in the merman's direction when he curled his lip before replying. "How brave of you to offer yourself, but your puny life is worthless to me. Lady Ariana must decide who will be left behind. I WILL have my revenge against King Midar. Either she remains to one day swing from a hangman's noose for the crimes she has committed, or she must suffer the rest of her days in Lunadar knowing she alone destroyed its legacy by casting aside her own daughter!"

Time seemed to slow down as one-by-one Ariana looked into the faces of those she cared for. There was no hiding the terror in her men's eyes as they awaited their fate. All they had ever done was what she asked of them, and now their fate rested in her hands.

Looking into the sea green eyes she had come to love, Ariana could see the tears much like her own reflected there. A soul in distress, Prince Kaspar could only look on helplessly as Lord Shemar held the life of his child in his hands. Ariana looked one more time at the sliver of moon resting on the water and knew what she had to do.

Bowing her head low in utter defeat, she said, "As you wish, Lord Shemar. I offer my life in exchange for the life of Candra and my men. I will hold you to your word my men will be returned safely to their families."

Lord Shemar made a mocking bow toward Ariana and said, "You have my word, milady. And as for your daughter, rest assured she will be in safe hands as I plan to make her my wife when she reaches the age of consent. She will be raised to know the dark ways of the Drundles.

There will be plenty of time to see how this one's power might show itself. Why, even Queen Naab might be interested to know I now control the future of Lunadar. And when the time is right, your daughter will become my wife so that our two realms will be joined together and Lunadar's destiny will be no more!"

Ariana and Prince Kaspar shouted out in anger, but the dark lord only laughed. They knew they were powerless to stop this from happening if Lord Shemar held the Cup of Notari, and now time was running out as the moonlight sat low on the horizon.

Through tears streaming down her face, Ariana's nails dug into the railing, and she refused to take her eyes off her child as her men climbed aboard the dark lord's ship.

She wanted to burn the memory of that angelic face into her heart. It almost felt like that very heart was being torn from her chest as Lord Shemar's ship slowly slipped through the portal and was lost to her.

Only then did Ariana allow herself to crumple onto the deck of her ship and let loose a cry of despair. All the king's sacrifices were in vain. All that she had strived to do in Lunadar's honor was gone in an instant, and her fate now lay in the hands of the gods.

EPILOGUE

Ariana didn't realize Prince Kaspar called to the sea creatures until she felt her damaged ship slowly being pushed toward Shanty's Cove by the same whales who came to her rescue once before. Little did it matter for her reason for living was torn from her. Soon the crumpled ship made its way to a secret inlet at Shanty's Cove. In a daze, Ariana felt herself being lifted into strong arms and carried to an outcrop of rocks near a sandy beach.

Slowly lifting her head to glance around, it took her a moment to realize this was the very place her men had set up camp for her many moons ago. The same place Prince Kaspar had first spoken of entwining their future lives together, and she only mocked him for speaking of such foolishness.

She turned tear filled eyes to find dark grey ones filled with worry staring back at her. Cupping her face in his sea roughened hands, Prince Kaspar slowly drew her to him before kissing her. For a moment, all they did was drink in each other's pain before Ariana pulled away from the prince. Anguish colored her words as she looked to the sea and whispered, "What have I done? Dear gods above! What have I done?"

Prince Kaspar took her ice-cold hands in his and tried to rub warmth back into them as he said, "Listen to me, my love. Lord Shemar is to blame for this, not you. Only the devil himself would make a mother choose between saving the life of her own child and the lives of her men or saving herself."

Ariana slowly shook her head. "No, I am somehow to blame for the gods' wrath raining down upon my people. This is my punishment for arrogantly believing I could become a better leader of Lunadar than my father ever was. There is some truth to Lord Shemar's words. The gods have delivered the life I am now forced to live in repayment for all the pain and suffering I have brought to the people of this world. Now it will only be a matter of time before I really do swing from the hangman's noose. Then I will have died twice in my daughter's eyes."

Anger and frustration tempered his words as Prince Kaspar forced Ariana to look at him. "Who is this whimpering woman sitting before me? Surely not the fearless leader of Lunadar to whom I've pledged my heart! Nor is she the feisty spirit who refused the betrothal of a sea devil until he proved worthy of her love.

Now is not the time to allow doubts to overrule what we both know to be true. The blood of a mighty king flows through you and he would be ashamed to see his daughter behaving in such a manner. He taught you to be strong. Now it is your turn to prove to him you know how to be brave as well!"

"And how do you suggest I do that? Lord Shemar has taken everything from me. I cannot even fathom living if I can no longer gaze upon my child's face ever again!"

Prince Kaspar reached out to gently touch the medallions hanging around Ariana's neck. "But you will have a way until I can figure out how to return you to Lunadar."

Ariana glanced at the strong fingers stroking the metal and realized the prince might be right. Removing one of the precious relics from her neck, she placed it in Prince Kaspar's hands before placing her own hand over his. She looked into his eyes and said, "Of course, you could be right. Lord Shemar does not know the power behind these relics. If there was a way to get this medallion to Candra then I would be able to watch over my child, even when I am not by her side."

"Exactly. I make a solemn vow to you, Ariana, that I will somehow find a way to see Candra receives this gift from her mother. And it will become my heart's desire and life's quest to find a way for me to remove you from this place and return you to Lunadar where you belong. We will be wed, and I will make Lord Shemar pay dearly for all he has done to those I love!"

Prince Kaspar leaned in to kiss Ariana deeply once more before slowly sliding back into the surf. With tears in his eyes, the prince called out to Ariana one last time, "Remember well that kiss, my love, and think of me often. Do whatever you must to survive in this world and listen for the mermaid's song, for I will return to you as soon as I am able.

It tears my heart in two that I must leave you even for a moment, but I must return to Renndar and make plans for rescuing Candra from the dark lord. Mark my words, Ariana. Macklebee will have much to answer for by the time I am through with him. I will also make Lord Shemar pay dearly for all he has brought down on Lunadar and Renndar.

For those crimes alone, the gods also have my vow one day I too will have my revenge upon the dark lord and his Drundles!"

Ariana stared out to sea long after the prince had disappeared beneath the foam and long after the portal door had closed, bringing with it a darkness to weigh heavily on her spirit. Slowly making her way to their long-abandoned camp, Ariana took a deep breath and squared her shoulders. As Prince Kaspar had reminded her, she was indeed King Midar's daughter. She would do whatever was necessary to survive in this world until her prince could return for her, and they were homeward bound for Lunadar once more.

LUNADAR BOOK DISCUSSION QUESTIONS

1. What did you like best about the book? Least?

2. What other books did it remind you of?

3. Which characters in the book did your like best? Least? Why?

4. Share a favorite passage from the book. Why did this passage stand out to you?

5. Would you read another book by this author? Why or why not?

6. If you got the chance to ask the author one question, what would it be?

7. Which character in the book would you most like to meet? Why?

8. Which place in the story would you most like to visit? Why?

9. What do you think of the book's cover? How well does it convey what the book is about?

10. What artist would you choose to illustrate this book? Why kinds of illustrations would you include?

11. How well do you think the author built the worlds in the book?

12. Did the characters seem believable to you? Did they remind you of anyone?

About the Author

Donna L Martin has been writing for over fifty years. Her genres include poetry, picture books, historical fiction chapter books, young adult fantasy, and inspirational essays for anthologies. In 2010, her first story was traditionally published, and in 2017 Donna started researching how to become an indie author.

In 2018, she received the rights back to her debut picture book and decided to open her own publishing house. Since 2018, Story Catcher Publishing has released several books in a variety of genres. Many of these books have gone on to win local awards and 5-star ratings from nationally recognized organizations. There are plans to release many more books, and Donna now offers Author Services other indie authors as well.

Learn more about Story Catcher Publishing at (www.storycatcherpublishing.com), or follow Donna on Facebook (www.facebook.com/donasdays), to get updates on the next book in this series, LUNADAR Candra's Revenge, to find out what happens next to Ariana, Kaspar, and their daughter, Candra. Coming out in the fall of 2026!

www.ingramcontent.com/pod-product-compliance
Lightning Source LLC
Chambersburg PA
CBHW061059100726
47911CB00012B/306